JAKOB STERLING

Steven Blackwell

Jakob Sterling
Copyright © 2018 by Steven Blackwell

All rights reserved. No part of this book may be used, reproduced or transmitted in any form or by any means whatsoever; electronic or mechanical and including photocopying, recording or with any storage and retrieval solution; without exclusive permission, in writing, from the publisher, and/or the author.

Published, in Canada, by Steven Blackwell
steven.blackwell1010@gmail.com

This book is a work of fiction. Names, characters, places and all of the incidents are the product of the authors' imagination or are used fictitiously. Any resemblance to actual events, locales, or persons, living or deceased, is coincidental or has been approved by the individuals who are recognized within the credentials.

Production Credits
Jakob Sterling cover model: Tait Christenson
Photography: Soaring Like Eagles Photography
Gus Sigurdson | gubby316@yahoo.ca
Produced by: Steven Blackwell
Edited by: FirstEditing.com
Written, Designed and Published in Canada (2016 – 2018)

Tellwell Talent
www.tellwell.ca

ISBN
978-1-77370-543-9 (Paperback)
978-1-77370-544-6 (eBook)

JAKOB STERLING

Also by Steven Blackwell

The Pale Murphys

Sometimes the most dangerous energy is created from nothing much at all. The Sterling's certainly didn't deserve their brutal futures. They were a young, vibrant family with a hope for prosperity and a goal to strengthen their solid internal bonds.

But thirty-three years earlier, Charles and Marion Murphy unknowingly created a nightmare. A boy with a troubled conscience and a fulsome ego. A driven boy without remorse who had retaliation on his mind.

Setting a trap from the afterlife and holding both his family, and the Sterling's hostage, Jimmy Murphy was going to seek vengeance. And it would take the strength of the entire family, plus one, to quell the evil turmoil in the old Murphy house.

232 Birch

When we both saw the little boy outside, standing in the pelting rain. That's when I started to belief in ghosts. Not because she saw him, and not because I saw him, but it was because we both saw him at the same time. That's what made me a believer. And just when we thought we had it all figured out, the vision of a man, walking past our door and heading to the bedroom that our children slept in, changed everything. After ten long years, the riddle was beginning to make sense. We weren't alone at 232 Birch. We just wouldn't be clever enough to realize how many residents lived there along with us. Ghosts do exist! 232 Birch confirmed it.

Kim,

Thank you for your continued support!

Your friend,

Steve Blackwell

June 1/18

This one is dedicated to, perhaps, the hardest working and determined person that I know.
My sister,
Brenda Kolasa

1
A Day That Would Live in Infamy

November 3, 1937

IT was a frigid and lifeless day outside. Such an awful time for a senseless death. Mother Nature offered no reprieve, as the winter of 1937 was upon them like a pack of wolves. It was rumored to be a long and challenging season.

A distressed teenage boy stumbled off the school bus at the end of his driveway and made his way up the winding dirt path toward his front entrance. The distraught boy shuffled his feet, making long streaks on the frost-covered ground and he stared down at his boots. His emotions were muted at best, and he seemed to be on a deliberate and focused mission.

This boy was a strapping young man; big for his age. He had a scowl on his face that would intimidate the dead and he didn't seem too interested in the glorious wonders of his front yard that contained spruce, elm, and oak trees. All were covered in a glistening layer of pearly white snow. The moans from the thick breeze wouldn't break his stride.

Finding the family's hidden key from underneath the dead potted petunia that proudly sat on the doorstep, he opened his front door and entered the warm confines of his house. He walked lethargically to the fireplace and threw his book bag down on the granite hearth. He knew that he was all alone, and for some strange reason this triggered his guilty conscience. He was seventeen years old and an only child. His parents wouldn't be home for an hour or so.

After helping himself to a cold glass of milk, the boy walked to the basement's entrance and opened the door. It creaked at the hinges and once fully ajar, displayed the obscure and hollow atmosphere below. He pulled the string with his right hand, illuminating the space below and descended into the bottom of the house. Once there, he scanned his surroundings and instinctively looked toward the room that, at one time, not too long ago, contained his grandfather's large metal World War One box. It had been missing for three months now and it devastated the family, as it contained a valuable inheritance in which the stubborn patriarch of the family was far too obstinate to transfer to a secured bank vault. The boy knew, all too well, what had happened to the box, and the stinging guilt suffocated him, as he changed direction and re-located to the far corner of the uncomfortable basement. Still quite dejected, the young man looked down onto the bare concrete floor and fixated on a long, one-inch thick braided rope that his father was using to rope off the family cemetery in the back yard. The boy grabbed the end of the rope and dragged all seven feet of it up the stairs and into the living room.

Once sitting on the chesterfield, he flipped the end of the rope in his hand, bending it into a magical loop and then straightening it out again. The crestfallen boy placed the rope on the coffee table in front of him and shaped it into the letter 'C'. Then, he formed an 'S' shape and squeezed the three sides of the rope together, where he pinched them tightly. As if he had practiced it before and with little hesitation, the boy took the end of the original 'C' and began wrapping it around the pinched space. *One, two, three, four...* the boy continued with a purpose and was undistracted. *Ten, eleven, twelve, thirteen...* and then he was content leaving an eight-inch loop at the end.

After tying a knot and securing the wrapped line, he slowly stood up and proceeded to the side entrance door. Still wearing his soiled boots, he dragged the interwoven rope behind him, outside and into the cold, late afternoon temperatures. Now he seemed to have a rejuvenated and unaccustomed confidence in his step, he walked around to the side of the house and into the family's massive backyard. Dark clouds moved in from the west and even more snow was forcing its way through them, but the boy was not deterred.

The rear of the property was as spectacular as the front and shared its plentiful foliage throughout. All seemed peaceful and secure, but bare and uninviting at the same time. Stopping for a moment and taking three enormous breaths, the boy focused on the massive oak tree in the back corner of the yard. He then made a B-line toward it and shifted his eyes, first to the right to look at the family plots, where his grandfather and grandmother were buried, and then to the left, where he saw his father's large wood chopping block. Shivering from the wind, he walked over to the block of wood and kicked it over onto its side. He then started rolling it with his foot to the corner of the yard.

The imposing oak tree was a sentimental landmark. He has spent countless hours there with his father, when he was younger, playing on the tire swing that still hung by an old, filthy piece of rope, and was protected from fraying by a thick rectangle of burlap. The boy dropped his rope at the base of the tree and sat on the ground. He hung his head and reminisced about the conflict that he had endured with his father, only a week earlier. His father was drunk and told him, quite adamantly, that if he missed his curfew ever again, he would break every bone in his body, so he could never play football again. Sinking further into his depressive memories, he remembered exactly how his livid father sounded when he was being scolded, and could still feel his saliva as it left his screaming mouth and sprinkled onto his face.

Then he glanced to the west side of the tree. A frozen moss had covered the spot where he had dug a huge hole. The boy knew that he was responsible for his family's sad misfortunes. He just couldn't face up to his actions. He would not be held accountable for his thieving act, or the shameful and emotionally excruciating encounter that he had with his tipsy father. Hundreds of thoughts clouded the teenager's brain, and his eyes glazed over with weariness.

Without further ado, the boy rolled the thick chopping block to the outside branch that secured the tire swing. He stood upon it and used his pocket knife to cut the swing free. It fell and landed on the frozen ground, bouncing once and rolled in a circle, coming to a rest close by. The boy stepped down from the block and grabbed his hand-crafted rope, and then stepped back on to the block of wood. After tying the rope tightly to the branch, using a clove hitch knot, he turned to look at the backside of his house once more. Without remorse, and perhaps only releasing a single tear that rolled down his cheek, the fragile boy placed the loop over his head and around his neck. He cinched it up tight and then held his breath. He was cold and afraid, lonely and confused, but he could see no other way out. His father surely hated him and his mother was always busy. Too busy for him it seemed nowadays. The boy closed his eyes tightly and counted to three in his clouded head. With one final gulp, he kicked the wooden block away and fell violently, albeit only twelve inches or so. His legs quivered for an instant, and then they became still. The multiple swallows in the yard appeared to postpone their song, and all was quiet once again.

Twenty minutes had passed since the inconceivable deed in the backyard when a blue 1929 Chevy pick-up truck rolled onto the long driveway and continued forward, toward the side of the house. Inside the truck was a cantankerous young man and a beautiful, but bashful woman. They were the boy's parents, and absolutely nothing could have prepared them for the life changing events that they were about to painfully endure.

"Charles, you'll just have to accept that he's almost a man now. I think he's ready to make his own decisions and become more independent. You just can't keep pressuring him to succ-"

"What in the hell is that?" Charles squinted into the backyard from his driver's side vantage point. Once he had rolled up to his regular parking spot beside the house, his wife, Marion, followed his sightline.

"What's that in the tree Charles?" She was now on the same page. "What's happened to the swing? What is that Charles?" The object of their attention swayed slowly in the breeze, and Marion's brain tricked her into some sort of hallucination.

Charles put the truck into neutral and turned the ignition off, but before he could speak, Marion continued with panic in her voice.

"There's a man in the tree Charles! A man, there's a man in the tree!"

Swinging his driver side door open, Charles could see now and it crushed him before he could react. "Jesus Christ. Jimmy?" Charles bolted toward the backyard corner as Marion got out of the truck and stumbled to follow him. Her chilling screams could have shattered the eardrums of mortals, and they echoed throughout the neighbourhood as she finally realized what she was witnessing. Numbness was soon to follow.

The parents sprinted, as fast as they could, but they never seemed to get closer to the boy swinging gently from the branch. They just kept running and time cruelly seemed to pass them by. Eventually though, Charles made it to the imposing oak and grabbed his son around the waist, trying to lift him and relieve the pressure around his neck. His feet slipped on the frozen ground and he struggled to maintain his balance. Each second proved to be an eternity. Like a never ending tunnel with no lights for as far as the eye could see.

"Jimmy? No!" Marion Murphy screamed as she watched her husband. "No! No... Jimmy!? Jimmy!? Oh God, please, Jimmy?"

A Day That Would Live in Infamy

Charles also yelled out his son's name, but there was no response. He cringed from the weight of the teenaged boy and looked up to the enormous branch, trying to figure out a way to release his son. He realized that he could not reach the branch from where he stood, but quickly scanned the ground with his eyes. There, he saw Jimmy's pocket knife and the wooden chopping block that his son had kicked aside in the last desperate moment of his life. He lowered his boy's body until he hung by the rope, once again, and reached down to pick up the knife. Moving the chopping block into the right place, Charles screamed his son's name, over and over; Marion shuddered with dread. Her disbelief of the terrifying situation caused her extreme internal pains, and she fell to her knees.

Charles stood on the block and feverishly sawed away at the thick rope above Jimmy's head. Once the blade had made it three quarters of the way through, the old rope snapped, and Jimmy's lifeless body crashed onto the firm ground where he rolled to his mother's kneel. His eyes were wide and appeared to call out for help. Marion screamed louder than before and could see that her baby was dead. Their minds raced and the memories of their son were prevalent.

The two shattered parents worked on Jimmy to try and revive him, but it was no use. He was gone and they yelled into his blue face as tears flowed, contemplating the reasoning behind his helplessness. Their son had taken his own life, at such a tender and youthful age, and it was far beyond devastating for the Murphys. The agony from the ordeal seemed to summon an anger that immersed the Murphy couple into a poisonous swamp of negativity. Their only son was dead and the sight of him swaying from the tree would never leave their minds until the day they died. It resonated like a drum through the cool breeze, and created a truly intimidating resentment that would transform the distant future, in a very precise and truly ominous manner.

2
A Continuing Saga

July 17, 1980

"BARBARA, wake up." Donald commanded his wife to snap out of her medicated sleep. "We're almost at the hospital Barb. Wake up now. Hang in there, honey."

The ambulance squealed down the busy main street of Clover Springs. Its sirens shrieked and paramedics quickly worked on stabilising Barbara Sterling. It was too early for the new addition and Donald, who rode along and held his wife's hand, knew it all too well. The rest of the family stayed behind at their new home. Richard watched his concerned sisters as they awaited some good news about their mother's delicate condition.

Barbara wasn't familiar with her surroundings, and was still a bit drowsy, but soon gained her wits and started to panic, attempting in vain to kick her feet that were strapped to the thin gurney.

"Donald, I've just had a horrible dream! No... no, it was a nightmare, really."

Donald leaned over his wife. "It was just a dream, Barb. Don't worry about that stuff now. You have to concentrate on your breathing. Is the pain still bothering you like it was earlier?"

"Donald, the dream was about Jimmy Murphy."

"Jimmy Murphy? Donald hesitated and anxiety crossed his face. "Why are you thinking about Jimmy Murphy, Barb? His evil is behind us, once and for all. There's no reason to fear him any longer."

The paramedic in the back of the ambulance raised his eyes and then squinted, confused by the couple's exchange. The recent events with the Sterling family had not made it through to the mainstream media and most accounts were kept appropriately secretive. Even the extraordinary Maria Prescott, who quelled the evil in the Sterling's old house, was sworn to a stringent degree of confidentiality.

"Barbara," Donald continued, "why are you so worried about everything? You're in a good place. These are the same people who looked after Rich when he was sick, remember?"

"It was so frightening Donald, and it was all about Jimmy... when he hun-"

Donald interrupted her, "Stop it now, Barbara. Forget about Jimmy Murphy and concentrate on this special little gift that you're bringing into this world. Jimmy Murphy is a thing of the past and so is that evil energy that interfered with our lives."

Barbara arrived at the hospital by quarter past one in the afternoon. She had calmed down a bit, but now feared that something was terribly wrong with her baby. She couldn't feel her child kicking, or moving at all for that matter. The paramedics removed her on a gurney from the back of the ambulance and rushed her into the emergency entrance while Barbara rubbed her stomach. Donald ran alongside consoling his worried wife.

Barbara managed to speak up again, despite her medicated state. "You realize that it's almost been three years, to the day, that Richard had his accident?" And with that news, Barbara began to hyperventilate.

"Breathe slower, Barb. Breathe slower. You're going to be alright. You just need to keep your breathing normal. You've done this before, Barb, you're a fighter. Don't ever forget how special you are to me and the kids." Donald felt light headed and his eyes periodically glazed over with tiny black dots. Barbara began to breathe ordinarily again, but opened her mouth wide, and cried out in pain.

Doctor Collins met the medical personnel at reception and barked orders at the paramedics to take Mrs. Sterling, immediately, to operating room number two. He motioned for Donald to wait outside of the room and charged in, followed by three nurses and an intern. Donald watched through the window at the top of the door as the specialists transferred his struggling wife onto the delivery table and began preparing sharp needles and supplies to comfort her. Another nurse approached the door and asked Donald to move aside, but he made a quick gesture and stopped her by holding out his arm, demanding an answer.

"I need you to tell me what's going on. Please, you need to tell me if my wife is going to be okay. What's happening in there? Is there something that you're not telling me? Now isn't the time for secrets."

"Please sir," the nurse pleaded, "let me through. I can't tell you the status of Mrs. Sterling if you don't allow me to pass."

Donald thought quickly about his actions and pulled back his arm, allowing the nurse to enter the room. She certainly understood his concern so she hesitated and tried to give him some comfort.

"Please, Mr. Sterling, have a seat over there and the doctor will give you an update as soon as possible." She swung open the door and rushed over to Barbara.

Donald continued to watch as his mind wandered to a darker place, not long ago, when he was visiting his son in the same hospital. He thought of the old house and its commanding presence. The backyard oak tree and the history that surrounded it was fresh in his mind and it started to make him sick to his stomach. The family had been through enough, he thought. Surely, their ill-fated luck wouldn't continue. *It couldn't* he thought, *could it?*

He remembered the challenge of his own sickness. A horrible and devastating period, which threatened the very livelihood of his loving family. Pushing his glasses up his nose, he slowly backed away from the door and turned toward the chairs in the waiting area. He scanned the area and saw a vending machine supplying coffee so he deposited a quarter that he dug out from his light tan slacks and waited for it to finish before adding two sugar cubes and taking a seat.

After twenty-two minutes, Doctor Collins came out of Barbara's room and approached the concerned husband.

"Mr. Sterling." He reached out his hand to guide Donald away from the small crowd. "Please, come with me. I have an update for you. Let's go somewhere a bit more private, if you don't mind."

The two men walked around the corner and into an empty hallway.

"Mr. Sterling... do you mind if I call you Donald?" He waited for the worried husband's approval and continued. "Donald, Barbara has been sedated. She's in early labour and actually has the urge to push already, but we've given her something to combat that. She's sleeping rather comfortably for the moment. I would suggest that we let her rest for an hour or so. Do you have something that you need to take care of? Barbara was asking about the kids. Go and see them, Donald." *Just let us do our work here, will ya?*

"What about the baby, doctor? How's the baby? Barbara is really worried about the baby." *As she should be.*

"The baby seems quite fine. We're all hearing a nice strong heartbeat and it doesn't seem to be in any distress at the moment. Go and see your family. Bring the children back with you in an hour or so. I'll be able to give you some more news then, okay?"

Donald nodded and walked toward the pay phone at the end of the hall. He rolled a filthy dime into the coin slot and dialed his home number. His second oldest child, Mary, who was about to turn fifteen, answered the phone at their new family home in

Clover Springs. Anticipating her father's call and an update on her mother's condition, she snapped up the receiver.

"Hello?" Mary asked. "Dad, is that you?"

"Yes honey, it's me. Let me have a quick chat with your brother please."

"How is Mom? Is Mom okay, Dad?" Mary was quite concerned and knew that her mother's delicate state was no laughing matter.

"Your mother's just fine, honey. The baby is good too. It's still in mom's tummy. She's resting right now, so I'm going to come home and then we can all come back here together. But I have to take a taxi so I want to ask Rich to get some things ready. Can you please get him for me?"

"Oh, I can get the things ready, Dad. That's no problem. Just tell me what we need and I'll get Amanda and Richard to help me. Even Misty will help. She's looking forward to the new baby too."

"Of course you can, sweetheart. I often forget just how grown up you're getting. Such a smart, beautiful young lady. My apologies, sweetie. Get a sharp pencil and a piece of paper, okay, Mary? I'll tell you some things to write down and then you and your brother and sister can get it ready… deal?"

"Deal!" Mary answered excitedly. "I can't wait to see Mom and my new brother or sister. I'll be right back and you can tell me what you need."

Donald took a taxi cab back to his home on the far southern end of Clover Springs. He paid the driver, plus tip, and entered the house where his three children were ready. Proud Mary had followed her father's instructions flawlessly.

"Dad, how's Mom?" Richard asked. "Here's your keys. She was in a lot of pain when the ambulance came, Dad."

"Mom's a little woozy from the medication, son." He looked at his youngest, Amanda. "Mom's resting now and then she will probably have the baby soon."

"I put Misty in the backyard Dad. She's resting under the wishing well. I don't think she really knows what's going on."

The four Sterlings all headed out to the crimson-coloured van and made their way to the hospital. An hour had swiftly passed since Donald left his wife to pick up his kids. The family had just entered through the emergency doors when Doctor Collins intercepted them and pulled Donald away from his children.

"Donald, something peculiar has happened."

Donald peered at the doctor and then scanned the room, looking for answers. "What's peculiar, doctor? What do you mean?"

"Barbara woke up Donald. We sedated her, but she woke up hysterical. She was screaming your name at first, like she was having a nightmare or something like that. Then she started up again and she was blaring 'Jimmy…Jimmy…Jimmy!' It was quite concerning to everyone in the hospital, but then she calmed down and asked for you and the children again."

"Can I see her? Can we all go in and see her? She needs her family right now."

"Yes, you can go and see her now, but not for long. You should know that we've given your wife an epidural. She's completely numb from her waist down to ease her pain. The delivery is imminent."

"Thank you." Donald looked over to his children. "Come on guys, let's go and see mom. We can't stay in the room long because mom needs her rest, but you can all go in for a minute and say hi."

Richard, Mary, and Amanda began to follow their father and Doctor Collins, in a single file, but the physician stopped them once more, turning to address Donald like he was afraid to proceed.

"Donald…we were running some tests and the baby's heartbeat seems a little sporadic. It just happened, all of a sudden, and now we may need to perform an emergency C-section on Barbara to safely bring the baby into the world." Doctor Collins looked over to Richard. "Hi Richard, you're looking well. I think that platinum blonde hair of yours makes you look distinguished and smart."

"Thank you, doctor," Richard responded. He reached up and ran his hand through his freshly cut hair. "I'm starting to get used to it, I guess."

Finally, the family made their way to Barbara's room and opened the door where she lay motionless on the bed. She cracked a smile and her eye's widened at the site of her cherished ones. Unfortunately, Barbara had something on her mind and it plagued her thoughts.

"The doctor says I may need surgery to deliver the baby." A tear rolled down her cheek as she spoke slowly. "There's something wrong with the baby's heartbeat."

"Don't worry yourself, honey." Donald tried to comfort his wife. "They know exactly what they're doing here. You're going to be just fine." He repeated these words to her over and over; it made Barbara feel sick to her stomach, but she never let on. She remained as strong as she possibly could, for her children.

"Yeah, Mom, you're going to be back on your feet in no time," Richard spoke up, "Like Dad says. Soon it'll be all over and we can go back home with our new brother or sister. Is there anything that we can get for you, Mom?"

Barbara shook her head slightly and reached out her hand to her eldest child.

"Come here and see me my dear," Barbara spoke softly. "You've grown into such a good young man. I want you to know that if anything was to happen to me, I'm going to need you to keep a close eye on your sisters. And help out your father... do you understand? And of course, the new baby. You have to help out everyone, okay? You're the miracle child son. You are so precious to me and your dad."

Richard grasped his mother's hand tighter and shook his head. "No, Mom. Nothing is going to happen to you. Don't talk like that. Soon we're all going to have a brand new baby to look after. You're the best, Mom."

"Mommy," Amanda interjected, "Why do you think something is going to happen to you? Your baby won't let anything happen to you. The baby will protect you."

Barbara smiled and stretched her hand out to her little girl. When she was near, Amanda rested her head on her mother's belly and

Barbara stroked her long brown hair. It was a special time for the youngest. She couldn't wait.

"You, my dear, have nothing to worry about. You are my special guardian angel. I'll always be near you, no matter what." She gently kissed Amanda's forehead and the nine-year-old smiled, closed her pretty eyes, and daydreamed about her mother's thoughtful and hopeful promise.

"And you…" Barbara waved over her middle child, Mary. "You're going to be a big sister again. I'm so proud of you. I hope that you don't forget that."

Mary leaned in to her mother. "You are the strongest woman that I know, Mom. Everything I've ever learned about being a good big sister, I've learned from you."

"Uhhh, what about me?" Donald chimed in.

"You know what I mean, Dad." Mary made no attempt to rescind the complement to her mother, and never took her eyes off Barbara.

The Sterlings all stood around, sharing their love with one another. They continued to heal after the horrific events that took place at the hands of the Murphy family. For once, and after many years, it seemed that everything was going to turn out just fine. But it was about then, that Richard Sterling looked up to the ceiling tiles and felt an overwhelming queasiness, which was accompanied by an instantaneous and throbbing headache.

3
End of a Legend, Beginning of a Nightmare

July 17, 1980

The lights in the hospital room flickered and everyone looked up toward them. No sooner had a nurse come in to the room when Barbara let out a dreadful scream and arched her neck toward the ceiling. The heart monitor that was hooked up to Barbara started beeping and panic ensued throughout the room.

"Donald," the doctor barked at the confused husband, "you all have to leave the room now."

"I'm not going anywhere, God dammit, my wife needs me." Donald was standing his ground as Barbara's delicate condition continued to deteriorate.

The doctor commanded, "Nurse Johnston, please take Mr. Sterling out and scrub him for surgery. You'll just make her sicker Donald. Go with the nurse."

"Yes, Doctor Collins." The nurse followed the order and grabbed Donald by the arm.

End of a Legend, Beginning of a Nightmare

"Surgery? What's going on? Why does she need to have surgery?"

"I told you that we may need to perform an emergency caesarean section on Barbara. Please hurry."

Donald looked over to his desperate and suffering wife. "Barb, it's going to be okay. I'll be right here."

With that, Donald and the children were hurried out of the delivery room. Doctor Collins and the nurses sedated Barbara, once again, preparing her for the fairly standard procedure. Barbara cried out uncontrollably, but her pains began to fade, as the quick acting drugs took effect.

Once Donald returned, sterile and clothed for surgery, he ran to his wife's bed side once again. She was barely conscious, but managed to open her eyes enough to look at her husband. He cupped his wife's hand in his own and smiled at her. His very presence seemed to offer a level of relaxation to his disheveled wife.

"You're right here," she said in a whisper, "Something is wrong, Donald. I can't feel anything. I'm numb all over."

"The nurses have made you comfortable, Barb. Soon we will have our new addition. Hang in there, honey."

As Barbara became a victim to the anaesthetics and fell asleep, Doctor Collins made the first precise incision and after a few moments of exploration, a senior nurse assisting the doctor made an astonishing announcement.

"Doctor, there's another one! There's two!"

"Holy shit. How did we miss this?" Doctor Collins questioned his professionalism. "Why are we just finding out about this now?"

Donald shook his head back and forth, trying to get some clarification from anyone in the room. "Two? What are you talking about? Two what? Somebody talk to me. Give me some answers here."

One of the nurses handed Donald a damp facecloth so he could place it on Barbara's forehead, but Donald, confused and nauseous, removed his glasses and patted his own face with it.

"It's twins Donald. There's two babies," the doctor confirmed. He yelled through a sheet raised to separate Barbara's face and Donald's view of the procedure. "Stay there, we will take care of things down here. This is truly unexpected Donald…really."

The doctor made a six-inch incision in Barbara's lower abdomen, and then another in her uterus. He then carefully removed the first child and Nurse Johnston quickly cut the umbilical cord. Another nurse snatched up the newborn and rushed it to a side table, removing obstructions from its nose and mouth.

"It's a boy! You have another son!" The doctor was more ecstatic than the father.

Donald was shaking. *Can they see me shaking?* He kept stroking his wife's cheek. She remained in her unconscious state. Doctor Collin's reached down again and removed the other child. This one was even smaller than the first and this time there seemed to be a truly grave issue that needed immediate attention. The doctor began sweating profusely and took a deep breath.

The baby's cord was wrapped around its neck and the medical staff worked feverishly to free the endangered life. Terror washed over the hospital's personnel and their faces became greatly concerned. The child was quickly cut free, but Barbara started bleeding un-expectantly and her heart monitor shrieked, as it alarmed again.

"What's happening?" Donald raised his voice, but his question simply blended in with the surrounding chaos. "Barbara? Barbara, can you hear me? You come back to me now okay? Everything is going to turn out just fine, honey." He wept. "It always does."

The second child was also a boy and they rushed him to the side table too. It was then that the first baby let out his first cry. It sounded like a growl, but brought smiles to the nurses' faces. Things were not so fortunate back at the delivery table. The bleeding was getting worse and Doctor Collins was having trouble controlling it.

"I need some more suction over here Miss Johnston. There's too much blood."

More alarms sounded and Donald couldn't contain his fright any longer. "Is she going to be alright, doctor? Her face is turning blue. What the hell is happening to my wife? Barbara? Barbara?"

End of a Legend, Beginning of a Nightmare

"Donald, please, I need you to leave the room. We have to try and stabilize Barbara. Go and tend to your children and let us do our work, I will come and get you once we have things in control here. Jesus Christ, Erica, get him out of here or things are going to get real bad, real fast."

"Barbara?" Donald heard the doctor's orders, but kept trying to reach his wife. "Barbara!"

With that, Nurse Johnston grabbed him by the arm and dragged him out of the delivery room and into the waiting area to calm down. His hands shook and he reached into his brown pants pocket to retrieve his anxiety medication. Once he had washed his pill down, he paced back and forth in the waiting room, his face glazed over with confusion and concern.

Back inside the room, a senior nurse announced a brief and agonising statement to Doctor Collins. "The second baby didn't make it, doctor." He nodded and sweat fell from his brow and directly into Barbara's open wound.

"I can't stop the bleeding. There's too much blood."

"Her blood pressure is falling rapidly, doctor." The assisting nurse delivered some more bad news.

"No, God dammit, don't do this, Barbara. Don't leave me now. You have a new baby who needs you."

Despite their best efforts, they couldn't replace Barbara's blood quick enough. His patient flat lined.

"Give me the paddles." He ripped the dividing curtain down and tried to shock Barbara back to life. Her body convulsed from the electricity pulsing throughout it, but she was unresponsive. A devastation had occurred.

After four failed attempts, Doctor Collins instructed the nurse to turn the irritating machine off and looked up to the clock on the wall.

"Time of death: 3:18." He reached down and pulled the sheet over Barbara Sterling's face, and then looked over to his assistant and paused. "I'll go and tell them. Get me an update on the surviving child please. I'll wait here for it. He'll need some good news." The nurse left through an adjoining swinging door where the first baby was taken for some additional tests. Within three minutes, she returned and updated the doctor on the child's condition.

Doctor Collins exited his office that was adjacent to the delivery room. He looked at Donald slumped over in the waiting room chair. Richard and Mary had gone to the hospital's cafeteria and Amanda lay asleep on the chairs beside him. Donald could sense the doctor's presence and turned slowly to meet his stare. He stood up and shuffled toward the doctor; tears welled up in his eyes. His lip quivered and he came within two inches of the doctor's face. Donald could tell, almost immediately, that the news was dire. She tried to warn him and his comforting acted like ear plugs. He felt it, deep down in his heart and pushed his glasses up the bridge of his nose. Then he beat the doctor to the punch.

"You don't have to say anything. I know what you're about to say. She's gone, isn't she? My Barbara's gone now, isn't that right? I never even got to say goodbye." Donald was slipping into shock.

The doctor reached out his hand and placed it gently on Donald's shoulder. "I'm so sorry, Donald. There was too much blood. We couldn't get it under control. She was too torn up inside. I've never seen anything like it before. We just couldn't stop the bleeding. We tried so hard. I'm so sorry. Where are your kids?"

"She's dead, isn't she doc? She died and left me here all alone now hasn't she?"

The doctor stared into Donald's eyes and a bead of sweat developed on his forehead. "Yes, Donald, I'm afraid so. I'm sorry. But I'm going to help you. We have good people who are going to get you through this. Our councillor, Lisa Passmore is quite proficient with these kinds of tragedies. I'll arrange for her to call you if that's alright with you."

Donald was peppered with different emotions. He whimpered and took off his glasses to wipe the tears from his eyes. And then he remembered something. Something that he should have never been forced to ever forget.

"What about the babies, doctor? How are the babies? When can I see them?" The agitated man tried to keep himself together.

Doctor Collins thought carefully about his answer for a moment. "The baby's fine Donald. The nurses are caring for him in the pediatric room. He will need to stay here for a while though. He is premature, but I assure you, he will have the best care available. You will need this time. Make arrangements for the burial of your wife and we will look after your son." The doctor couldn't think of anything past the deceased, second child, but wasn't about to deliver even more bad news to the dejected man so he kept it to himself. At least for a few stressful seconds.

"What about the other baby? Is it with the boy in the pediatric room? Is it a boy or a girl?"

"Donald, the other baby was stillborn. The umbilical cord was wrapped around his neck. It was another boy. I'm so sorry."

The next eight hours were a whirlwind for the Sterling family. The children were all told, one by one, that their mother had passed away during childbirth. Nothing was said to them about the twin brother. There was no need to give the kids more grief. The news was acknowledged in different ways by the three Sterling children. Richard was saddened greatly and cried briefly, but seemed to find some sort of comfort in the birth of his healthy brother. Mary was shaken and distraught. She lowered her head, but failed to shed a tear. Inside, she sheltered her pain and her helplessness was already quite noticeable. Amanda was heartbroken, but stayed relatively calm with the news of her mother's passing. She seemed to doubt the truth of the dire situation. Amanda did cry though and her emotions mimicked those of her two older siblings.

Barbara had no loved ones other than her immediate family. Her father died when she was quite young and her mother had passed in 1971, one day after little Amanda was born. Her only sibling lived across the Ocean. A sister, and they hadn't spoken to each other in more than fifteen years. The funeral's patron's would be few, but the loved one's that were there would surely cry enough for all.

The Sterling family all huddled together at home. The three children, their devastated father, and their loving pet, Misty, an adult golden retriever who sensed that something was very wrong once her mistress was not present. None of them knew how they were going to help each other through this horrible ordeal, but together, as a family, they were going to have to find out. The next few years would define the family's courage and resolution.

Now they would have an added responsibility to care for. Someone who would only be told about his mother: the bestselling author of many books; the resilient and independent mother who loved her children and never asked for anything in return. The new child would learn all about her eventually. Donald knew that the child would need to know about his mother. The child had already created a special internal bond with her and he would become perceptively curious.

And the baby would need a name. Donald encircled his kids with his arms and told them to think about a name for the baby. This would help take their minds off their mother for a moment. The children were happy to play the game. They continued to whimper, but this offered their mind a distraction, which noticeably shifted them to a more positive place. Amanda was the first to offer a suggestion.

"How about we call the baby Bart? It kind of sounds like Mommy's name." She wept louder for a moment.

Donald managed to chuckle through his grief, but stopped himself. "That's one idea for sure. Thank you, honey. Does anyone else have any ideas?"

Richard looked up and shared his brilliant idea. "We should name him something that honors the memory of Mom. Something from her ancestry maybe. Mom has a German heritage right? How about we name the baby Jakob? Jakob with a K! That's what Mom told me that I was almost named. But with a 'C' I think. Jakob with a 'K' would sure honor Mom's memory, don't you think guys?" There was a brief moment of hope and agreeance, but after that, no one spoke, and the Sterling family went back to a gut-wrenching mourning.

4
You Are Welcome

October 2, 1980

As autumn began, and the trees surrounding the Sterling's house displayed their copper-coloured leaves, Jakob had finally made it home. After seventy-six long days in the neo-natal ward, his entrance would be triumphant, and although the family continued to mourn over Barbara's sad and crushing passing, there *was* a pretty good reason to stay positive. Jakob would hopefully be the glue that held the family's broken pieces together at the seams.

Erica Johnston, a young nurse from the Clover Springs General Hospital, had brought the infant to his family and lay the sleeping child down in a bassinet in the living room before motioning for Donald to sit and chat. She could see the despair on the man's face and felt some animosity radiating from his stature. Erica had dark black circles under her eyes and her lips were chapped with small pieces of skin hanging off them.

"Thank you, Miss Johnston. I appreciate you and the other nurses looking after my boy for me. I wasn't really too worried knowing he was in good hands with you at the hospital."

Erica had a perplexed look on her face and peered around the room before addressing Donald.

"Where's the rest of your family, Mr. Sterling? Maybe they should hear what I have to say as well."

"It's just me here right now. Richard is living in the city, attending university. He's in his first year studying engineering. My two girls are both in school today. It's Thursday, but it feels like Friday. I can't keep the days straight anymore to tell you the truth."

The nurse understood, "It's quite alright Mr. Sterling. I wanted to fill you in on Jakob's condition."

"Condition?" Donald exclaimed. "What condition?" The young nurse could feel nervousness creeping in and it was starting to control the lost father of four.

"There's no reason to be alarmed, Mr. Sterling. I didn't mean it like that. What I mean is how he's been feeling and what we've noticed while he's been with us. He seems perfectly healthy to me. No need for any of us medical professionals to be concerned, anyway."

"Oh yes." Donald calmed a slight bit and pushed his glasses closer to his forehead. "Yes of course, please go on Miss Johnston."

A sudden ruckus arose from the basement area and it was Misty who came running up the carpeted stairs to join his master and their guest in the living area. Erica reached out and began stroking Misty's long golden mane.

"Oh, I just love dogs! Hi girl." She quickly looked up at Donald. "She is a girl, isn't she?"

Donald smirked and nodded at the nurse, motioning for his dog to lie down beside him on the floor.

"Mr. Sterling, your son, Jakob was born too early. He almost didn't make it because he was so small and..." she paused. "And his brother wasn't strong enough, but Jakob was. He was so strong and we've noticed just how strong he really is while he's been with us."

"What exactly do you mean?" asked Donald.

The nurse glanced over at the bassinet and a slight smile crossed her lips. "Jakob has very pretty eyes. His eyes are a beautiful shade of yellow. They pierce right through you, and you can't stay in eye contact with him for more than thirty seconds... a minute tops." She took a breath and looked at Donald with a purpose. "But you see Mr. Sterling...no one can. No one's able to."

Donald's mouth drooped open and he approached his sleeping son. "You're kidding right?"

"Mr. Sterling," the nurse continued, "there's more."

Donald turned and waited for her to speak again.

"Jakob's brain activity is off the charts. I've...We've never seen anything like it before. He cries for long periods of time and throws up a lot. I don't think he likes peas too much, but I've been instructed to feed peas to him and most of the time he throws up on me, or the floor." Erica appeared rather intimidated, all of a sudden. She perspired and her throat was dry.

"Okay, just a second here." Donald seemed confused. "What do you mean he cries for long periods? Doesn't every baby?"

"Not like this, Mr. Sterling. Jakob will scream bloody murder if he's not happy. And he doesn't seem to be very happy with me most of the time. But I really love him and I will miss him. I hope that I can visit him soon, and please let me know if there is anything that I can do to help you." She stood up to leave, and was suddenly uncomfortable with her surroundings, but Donald rushed over to her and gently grabbed her arm.

"Wait, Erica, please. That's it? That's what you wanted to tell me? My son cries and screams and throws up when he eats peas? He's strong and some sort of a 'Brainiac'? I don't understand. Why do I feel that there's something that you're not telling me?"

The young and pretty nurse became bashful and her inexperience in uncomfortable situations was apparent. "I'm sorry for your loss, Mr. Sterling." She headed to the front door and slipped her shoes on. Donald and Misty were right behind her. "I'll leave you with your new son now."

"Please, Erica, don't go. Stay and have some coffee. Tell me why you're so alarmed."

Erica looked toward the bassinet in the living room and then back to Donald's tangled stare. "I wish you luck, Mr. Sterling. You really have a lovely home. Take care." And with nothing further, away she went. Donald watched her as she walked down the sidewalk and then ran out of his sight. *Something was disturbing that girl*, he thought, but he wouldn't find out any further parallels and his mind reminded him of his new son, once again.

The tired and overwhelmed father glanced up at the clock on the wall and realized that his two girls would soon be arriving home on their school bus. Mary, his oldest daughter, was now in grade ten. She had just turned fifteen years of age and despite her mother's death, she continued to excel in her schooling. She had developed into the mother figure for the household and, even though she was forced into it far too early, she embraced the challenge and matured quickly with her added responsibilities.

Donald's youngest daughter, Amanda, was nine years old now and attended grade five at the historic Clover Springs elementary school. She emulated her mother's good looks, with long brown hair and a shiftiness in her eyes that reminded Donald of his beautiful wife. Amanda was still a child, and followed her older sister around, as she attempted to replicate her qualities.

Donald smiled as he thought of how lucky he was. His youngest son, asleep in the bassinet, had begun to stir, but remained napping. His oldest son, Richard, was to turn nineteen in February of 1981. Donald was so proud of him and the adversities that he overcame by the hands of the Murphy family, not so long ago. And now he was attending university in the city. He too, would be excited about officially meeting his new baby brother, but his schooling had made it difficult for him to visit over the last couple of months. As the blissful emotions overwhelmed Donald, for the first time in ages, he was reminded that, without his wife, it wasn't going to be that easy.

Donald knew that his life's priorities would need to change. He wouldn't be able to pursue his photography business as aggressively as he once did, and he wouldn't have his wife to depend on any more. This continued to sadden him, but he knew that it was his responsibility to step up and show his family that their quality of life would continue to be pleasant and lucrative.

As the memories of his late wife flooded his thoughts, Donald reached down and adjusted the yellow blanket that covered his son. He then turned and slowly walked to his wife's old office. The office where she had completed her final novel, just prior to her visit to the hospital in July of this year. He hadn't been in the room since then and finally built up the strength to proceed.

Donald opened the door and the immediate aroma of Barbara's perfume rushed out of the room. He stood with his eyes closed and took deep breaths. Pushing his glasses closer to his head, he sluggishly walked over to the wooden writing desk and chair that his wife used to sit in. He looked down on the ground and saw a letter-sized piece of paper. Reaching down to pick it up, he could see that it was the proud title page of Barbara's recently completed memoir. She had entitled it *The Pale Murphys* and Donald knew that the enormous pile of papers on the desk represented the chaos and terrifying ordeal that the family had faced, while residing in their old dwelling. The old Murphy house had now been destroyed by the city, but the memories would never subside. He took his right hand and placed it upon the stack of papers where his thumb began to fan the edge of the pages. His mind replayed the events of those days, and they were still as fresh in his mind, as his wife's tragic death.

His immediate memory was that of his son, Richard. He had gotten sick shortly after moving into the old house. Before the family could wrap their heads around his issues, he had endured a horrible and mysterious accident in the dark basement. The alleged accident resulted in his son slipping into a coma for just shy of two long years. Other than Richard's platinum blonde hair that he seemed to have inherited from the excruciating and lengthy ordeal, no one would ever guess that he had even undergone the wicked and painful experience. He held his head high and projected an admiral confidence.

Donald thought of Jimmy Murphy. The sad, disturbed teenager who took his own life, hanging himself in the backyard's tremendous oak tree. His spiritual energy that existed in the old house was the very same energy that hurt his son. He knew this now after a long period of time, as he falsely accused Jimmy's father for the pain, originally.

He knew that Jimmy's spirit had resided in his son's head and body. He was aware that the energy moved into him when Richard was no longer a challenge. And, even though many of his own experiences with Jimmy Murphy's energy was a blur, he knew that he had hurt all of the members of his family. Even his dog, Misty, who stood by him in the office wagging her tail and panting from the comfortable warmth of the house. His agonising misconducts were unwanted, but he was a prisoner to Jimmy Murphy.

Then Donald recalled the freakishly large, spiritual medium who was able to quash the resilient energy of Jimmy Murphy and remove it, once and for all, from his family's lives.

The entire painful story was laid out in front of him. He wouldn't be able to read it though. This would surely be the best way to honor his late wife and appreciate her memory, but he knew that this just wouldn't be possible. The story was told from the mind of Barbara Sterling and that may be far too much to bare. Then he came up with a great idea. The project was complete. He would just send the manuscript to his wife's publisher, in the city, and the final piece of work would become a memorial; her crowning achievement. It would be appreciated by her thousands of fans and readers who existed throughout the entire world. She deserved that. *At least that*, he thought. Donald gathered up the papers, smiled, and exited the office, closing the door behind him.

Just then, the front door opened and Amanda and Mary entered the house, having just been dropped off by their school bus. An excited Misty barked and ran to the door to meet them, brushing up against Amanda and almost knocking her small frame over.

"Hi Misty girl." Amanda stroked her pet.

"Hi Dad, how are you?" Mary looked lovingly at him.

Before Donald could respond, and still holding his wife's manuscript, Mary noticed her new baby brother in the bassinet. The child was waking up, and after taking off their shoes at the door, the two girls excitedly ran over to the infant's resting place in the living room. Amanda giggled at the thought of being a big sister.

"Hi girls, welcome home. How was school?" Donald walked over to join his daughters as they gawked at their new brother.

"Fine Dad," Mary confessed, but she was focused on Jakob and didn't have much interest in talking to her dad about her studies. "Hi little Jakob." She reached down and grabbed her brother's little finger. "Look guys, he's opening his eyes."

Jakob yawned and an unusual sound for a newborn left his mouth. He opened his eyes wide and seemed to target his father's stare, almost immediately.

"Wow, look at his eyes, Dad." Amanda was seeing her brother close up for the first time. "They're so yellow, don't you think? He kind of has eyes like a wildcat, doesn't he? They're kind of memorizing too aren't they? It kind of hurts my head to look at them for a long period of time to be completely honest."

Donald smiled and opened his mouth to speak. He never had a chance though. Jakob started to scream. He was loud and made Misty run into the kitchen for cover. The child never took his eyes off Donald, and the girls were shocked by their brother's lung capacity. Jakob had arrived, and despite his irritating howl and creepy stare, he was accepted and loved by Donald and the two girls.

He would be loved by his older brother too, when he got the chance to meet him. That would only be in a couple of months. Richard would return to Clover Springs for Christmas and finally, the new Sterling family would all be together. All except for Barbara. Her untimely loss would not be forgotten by any of them anytime soon.

5
A Shining Christmas Light

December 19, 1980

JAKOB was five months old already. And what a challenging five months it had been for the shaken Sterling household. Erica, the nurse who cared for Jakob, had warned about the child's temper and strong lungs. She was pretty accurate. Jakob had grown quickly and it would be difficult to recognize him as a pre-mature baby. Over the past two months, Jakob went through almost seven-hundred diapers. Mary was constantly laundering the cloth nappies that the boy used. He vomited on a daily basis and screamed on cue. He rarely cried anymore, but the horrid screams, most definitely, took precedence. The child also liked to squirm and fidget while being held. Mary had accidentally dropped him off the couch a week earlier, but Jakob, luckily, was not hurt. Just a bump on the head and another reason for an already atrocious attitude. Just like every other child, Jakob would have to learn some lessons the hard way.

Richard was home for Christmas. He was finding his university courses challenging, but was keeping his nose above water. He juggled his new friends with their unique and exclusive personalities, while, creatively defining his own independent strategies. Once he had arrived and was introduced to his baby brother, he was put in charge of handling Jakob.

The oldest child came out of the bedroom where he had just put his brother down for the night. He walked to the living room, where his father was stretched out on the sofa watching television and drinking a hot chocolate with whipped cream topping.

The living room had a small Christmas tree that sat in the corner of the room. It had been decorated mostly by Amanda, and was themed to her mother's memory. There was a picture of Barbara placed in the tree and it shone from the multi-coloured lights, blinking in succession. Mary had added some poinsettias and colourful garlands to the fixtures around the room and all was accomplished to surprise their older brother on his return home from his post-secondary schooling. *But he had immediate concerns...*

"Dad, I don't know why you haven't mentioned it to me, but there's something wrong with Jakob. He's not a normal kid. You can see that right?"

Donald put his newspaper down and pushed his glasses closer to his forehead. "There's nothing wrong with him, son. He's just a baby. That's how babies are. Why do you think he's not a normal kid?"

"It's the way he is, Dad," Richard was quick to respond. "It's his cold stare and his constant screaming. It's like he knows he doesn't have to scream, but he does it anyway. He stares right at me and screams like he enjoys aggravating me. His eyes burn, Dad. I have to look away sometimes. I even have to pretend that I'm just looking around for something. He just stares. And I've seen him stare like that at you too, Dad. He doesn't seem to stare right through Mary and Amanda. But he stares through us Dad. Why is that?"

"Rich, you have to understand, he's only a baby. He doesn't know what's right and what's wrong yet. He certainly can't choose to stare at one person, but not stare at another. Come on now, son, don't be silly. He's just a little boy, like you were once. I don't think he's out to get you."

Richard had no interest in arguing with his father. He felt that the accusations about his brother were justified, and wasn't afraid to let his father know how he felt. As tensions in the room escalated, the two girls entered the living room from the kitchen where they were having a light snack before going to bed.

Mary had an invite from friends to go out to a dance competition at the town hall, but backed out of it at the last minute with a stomach ache. Not exactly how she wanted to spend her Friday night, but her studies were far too important to her. She couldn't afford getting sick and missing too much school. She took her glass of water and walked over to her father to give him an affectionate kiss on the cheek.

"Dad, I'm going to bed now. I need to try and get rid of my tummy ache." Mary rubbed her belly and sighed.

"Me too, Dad." It was Amanda's turn. "Have a good night. I need my beauty sleep. That's what Mom used to say. Hey, can Misty sleep in my room tonight, Dad? She's pretty tired too, I think. I'll make sure and let her out if she needs to go."

"Sure," Donald snickered and motioned toward Richard. "Give your brother a hug goodnight girls. And remember, tomorrow's a big day. We're going for a sleigh ride around the town. Hopefully the weather cooperates. It'll be Jakob's first adventure outside of the house. That's what he needs. A bit of fresh air should brighten his spirits."

"Goodnight, Mary." Richard hugged his sister and then crouched down to hug Amanda. "Goodnight Dee-Dee. Hey listen, can you can look after Jakob tomorrow when he wakes up? Just until we go on this sleigh ride? He's tuckered me right out these last few days, and I think I could use a bit of a break. Is that okay with you?"

"Sure, Richard, no problem." Amanda stood tall in her flower-covered nighty. "I'll keep an eye on him tomorrow, and I'll show you how a pro does it. He's no problem for me."

Yeah," Mary followed up. "That's until he screams at you, right?"

Both of the girls chuckled and headed off to their respected bedrooms down the lengthy hallway.

It wasn't long before the clock read midnight, and as a light snow fell and glistened beneath the street lamp out front, the entire household slept.

The nursery was located in between the master bedroom, where Donald slept and the two girls' sleeping quarters across the hall. At approximately 3:17 a.m. an unusual noise resonated from Jakob's bedroom. The noise woke Amanda up and she lied in bed, clutching her covers, and listened intently. Hearing noises in the night was common place for the young girl, but it had been months since she had encountered something of this sort. The noise continued as a pulsating murmur from the room across the hall. *Surely the others could hear it as well.* After ten minutes, Amanda pushed her covers aside, waking up her pet golden retriever in the process, and placed her feet on the warm carpeted floor.

Misty quickly fell back asleep, as she didn't seem to be bothered by the strange noise coming from Jakob's room. But Amanda needed to investigate. After all, safety was certainly a pre-requisite for being a new big sister. She would have to be quiet to ensure that she didn't arouse the other family members, so she tiptoed out of her bedroom and into the dark hallway. The noise had stopped once she reached the hall, but Amanda's curiosity controlled her actions and her motivation caused her to open her younger brother's bedroom door. The door creaked, but when she slowed her pushing motion, it only squeaked louder.

Once ajar, Amanda quickly flicked the light on and was surprised to see that her brother was fast asleep and the noise had completely subsided. Amanda crept up to the side of the crib and listened to her infant brother breath. Each exhale sounded like the growl of a baby wolf, and his eyes moved, very rapidly, under his lids. Amanda scanned the room one last time before backing up to the door and flicking the light off. She closed the door and went into the bathroom to pee before heading back to her bedroom.

As she neared her room, Misty yelped and ran down the hall, into the living room where she continued around and bolted down the staircase and into the basement. Amanda was startled and wondered what could have spooked her dog so easily.

The youngest Sterling girl took the twelve steps needed to arrive at her bedroom's entrance. The light was off, but she had left it on when she had exited only minutes earlier. There was a bright illumination coming from her room. Before Amanda could verify the bright light, she could tell that the brightness was un-natural and electricity seemed to flow throughout the hallway. This had become, all too familiar.

Amanda entered her room with only a little fear and witnessed an amazing sight in the corner of her room. She couldn't make out the manifestation, but could tell that it was that of a human form. It hovered, about three feet from the ground and was void of any legs or feet. The top of the illumination was at least seven feet tall, and just avoided blending in with the bedroom's ceiling. Amanda stared in awe unable to take her eyes off the apparition.

Maybe she was sleep walking, or maybe the energy that persisted in their old house had somehow followed them to their new house. *How could this be?* Amanda thought. She saw Maria Prescott remove the spirit of Jimmy Murphy and she watched as her friend, Dortie, and the other Murphy family members were set free from their incarceration. She continued to watch as the light intensified in brightness and strength. Amanda's eyes grew to the size of suit jacket buttons and she opened her mouth, as she felt the need to speak.

"Who are you?" she asked. "You don't scare me, you know. Tell me who you are or I'm going to tell my Dad that you're here." The light had no reaction to the little girl's threat and Amanda made her next move. "You just wait here okay? I'll be right back, because I'm gonna get my Dad. He'll want to see you, I think."

With that, the glorious energy in the room weakened and vanished along with the electric waves that seemed to pulsate throughout the house. All was dark and quiet again. Amanda turned her bedroom light on, still breathing heavy, and went to the corner of the room where the light was displaying itself. Nothing was out of the ordinary though, so after a few minutes, the tired nine year old shut her light off and went back to her bed, pulling her covers high up to her chin and closing her eyes.

"A Christmas miracle," she said to herself, under her breath. But her thoughts plagued her and she failed to fall back asleep for another two hours.

At 5:19 in the morning, the household was woken by Jakob's screaming. Donald jumped out of bed and realized that Amanda was still sleeping when he stood between her and Jakob's room. The piercing scream didn't seem to faze her. Donald entered Jakob's room and swept the infant up in his arms, slinging him over his shoulder. The screaming continued and, before long, both Mary and Richard were up as well, scratching their heads and shuffling their feet.

"Shhhh, my little man. Are you hungry again? Or maybe you have a poop that needs changing. Your sister Amanda was supposed to look after that this morning, but I guess she's pretty tired." The child finally quieted down a little bit, once Donald presented a bottle that he took from a small refrigerator in the nursery. "There you go, my boy. That's all you wanted wasn't it? I have a funny feeling you're up now for a while, aren't you?"

"I'll take care of him if you want Dad." Mary offered her services and advised her father and older brother to go back to bed for a couple of hours at least.

"Are you sure, sweetheart?" Donald was relieved by the gesture. "That would be such a great help. Thank you." Mary took Jakob from her father's arms and the child seemed to unwind and calm down almost immediately. She took her little brother down the hallway and into the living room where she kicked Misty off the couch and lay down with Jakob on her chest. The rest of the family went back to bed and took advantage of Mary's generosity.

Before eight in the morning, the family all met in the dining room and gathered around the circular dining table. Jakob hung in his jolly jumper, bouncing up and down, and making grunting noises with each leap. Amanda was the last to join the clan, and had a somewhat disturbed look on her face when she entered the dining area. It was obvious that something was on her mind and she needed to get it off her chest.

"What's the matter with you?" Mary asked. "Weren't you supposed to look after J this morning?"

Amanda gained the attention of the entire family with her next words. They were words they never thought they would ever hear again, but it was un-stoppable and Amanda wasn't about to spare them the punishment.

"Last night I saw another ghost. It was in my bedroom and it was looking at me. It wasn't the Murphy ghosts though. It was a different kind of ghost. It was above the ground like the other ghosts, but it was very different."

The Sterling family's mouths all dangled open and Donald found the strength to challenge his daughter.

"What are you trying to tell us, Amanda? The ghosts are gone remember? There's no more ghosts. Not here in this house."

"But I saw it, Dad. It was in my room and it was similar to the old house, with the lights and the-"

"You were dreaming Dee-Dee. That's all it was. It was just a dream. Now don't bring it up again. We don't need any more ghost stories in our lives, all right? No more. I can't handle anymore ghosts right now."

All of the talking stopped after that, but Donald knew that his daughter was probably telling the truth. The claim was from recent experience too, and this caused great alarm.

6
Haven't We Met Somewhere Before?

March 10, 1981

JAKOB'S first Christmas swiftly came and went. The family rejoiced over their new addition, while paying a somber tribute of respect to their fallen mother and wife. Jakob himself hadn't caused too many challenges for the Sterling family. Now, just seven days shy of eight months old, Jakob's excessive screaming had lessened. He still made the snarling noises that had become a comedic staple in the family's talk track, and he vomited more than the family expected, but he was a Sterling, and he was loved. His eyes wouldn't be so difficult to look at anymore either. It was like he had already punished them enough and he gave permission.

Amanda hadn't experienced anymore anomalies in or around her bedroom. She felt that talking about it wasn't appreciated by her father, but something still intrigued the young girl. She needed some further clarity about her visitor. Maybe the light was related to the manifestations in the old house, or maybe it was something completely different.

The winter's presence was disappearing. It had been a mild season this year, all things considered. Donald had even taken on a couple of new photo shoots and the girls would take some more responsibility while looking after their younger brother.

Richard had returned home to his lonely one-bedroom apartment in the city. He focused on his studies and called frequently to check on his family members in Clover Springs. During his last call, he spoke about a headache that lasted throughout his visit at Christmas. Mercifully, it had gone away when he got back home. There was something that didn't add up though. He wasn't quite sure.

On this particular Tuesday, the girls had just caught the bus for school and Donald was preparing Jakob for an early spring walk around town. Jakob was putting up quite the fuss and wasn't too interested in cooperating with his father's wishes. Squirming and barking at Donald, the child would make direct eye contact him every chance he had. Donald had even admitted to Richard, on the telephone, that his continuous staring seriously creeped him out and wondered why Jakob did not do it when he interacted with the girls. At least he didn't notice.

After loading a disobedient Jakob into the stroller and attaching Misty's leash, Donald threw on his brown suede coat, locked up the house, and picked up the daily newspaper from the step before making their way down the sidewalk.

Forty-five minutes of walking passed by like a bolt of lightning. Donald had almost made it to the other end of town. He slowed his pace as he turned his son's stroller onto a very familiar street. It was their old street. The street that Jakob had been conceived on. And at the end of it, the fabled property which once contained the house that Donald, Barbara, Richard, Mary, and Amanda had lived in for more than three years.

But the troubled house wasn't there anymore. It had been demolished by the town after the Sterling's moved out. The town's dignitaries had long unfinished business with the house and property alike, and they finally got their way. The town's council had communicated their dismay with the fact that the Sterling's agreed to have the massive oak in the corner of the property sawed down. It was a task headed by the psychic medium who helped the family so badly, during their time of despair. By the time the deed was done, the town hadn't caught wind and couldn't repeal.

Donald became insistent on seeing what progress had been made on the property. The council had promised a huge, wooded park area. It was a big part of their 'beautification' project. He pushed the stroller down the sidewalk, making a slight dog leg to the right before viewing the site line to the old property. Jakob had started to fidget and Donald knew he would have to be quick and start making their way home for lunch.

When Donald, Jakob, and Misty made it to the corner lot, they paused and just looked. Donald was astounded at the transformation. The old winding driveway had been converted to a beautiful stone walkway, surrounded with freshly planted flowers of many different colours. The trees that were once part of his front yard remained and benches and fancy picnic tables were placed strategically throughout. Donald looked to where the house used to be and saw there were new trees planted and a garden with a pond had been erected. The massive iron fence and gate had been taken down and it certainly didn't look anything like the *'freak show'* that he had been told about by the towns people and then actually witnessed firsthand. There were so many memories that came flooding back to him and he saw his lovely Barbara, in his mind, everywhere.

He continued pushing the stroller with one hand as he pulled his dog with the other. He wanted to go into the park and look at the makeover, but Misty had become defiant. She dug in her heels and sat on the ground, making it difficult for Donald to continue forward into the park.

"Come on girl. Let's go." He tugged at the leash even harder and Misty's collar rode up around her head as she whimpered. "Okay fine, if you don't want to come in with us, you can just stay right here then."

Donald tied up his dog to the sign announcing the name of the park. He secured his pet and looked up to the sign. It read, *Edward John Murphy Park*. This made Donald dreadfully uncomfortable and he found it difficult to breathe for a moment. The Edward Murphy they were referring to was the man who built the house and landscaped the property. He was Charles Murphy's father, and Jimmy Murphy's grandfather. Regardless, Donald rolled his son up the pathway toward the new park. Misty barked for attention, but soon it was quiet, as only a few people occupied the green space.

As Donald continued up the path, he recognized the far corner of the park. The massive stump from the fabled oak tree was still there. They had made it into a picnic table and surrounded it with wooden blocks for seats. It had been sanded and lacquered, but something from the past still remained. The eerie sentiment around the stump still persisted. This was the stump that held the tree that Jimmy Murphy hanged himself in. This was the place that riches were buried and the place where tragedy caused an ominous and fearful haunting. But despite the freakish aura, Donald decided to face his demons and sit down at the majestic stump.

He removed the folded newspaper from the basket in the bottom of the stroller. When he stood up, Jakob was staring at him, directly and with a purpose. Donald reached up and pushed his glasses toward his face. He matched his son's gaze and tried to out-stare him, helping to release the tension between them.

"What's up, champ? You wouldn't remember this place. There's really no good memories here anyway. But this is where you originally came from. I sure wish your mother was here to see this."

He looked over to where the house used to be in hopes of catching some sort of a supernatural glimpse of his stricken bride, but there was nothing except a small pond with two mallard ducks, and a couple of benches. A few saplings had been planted strategically, and serenity reigned. He turned back to Jakob who continued his penetrating stare into his father's eyes. Donald felt slightly intimidated.

"No need to worry about it. It's a nice spring day and I didn't even need my coat. What do you say we just kick back here for a few minutes so Daddy can read the newspaper?" He pointed toward the entrance of the park. "Misty can wait for a few minutes. She was too scared to come in here. I guess she has some pretty frightening memories of this place too. I can't believe she remembers it from the way it used to be."

Donald Sterling had a seat and flipped open the town's daily rag. Immediately, an article on the front page grabbed his attention. He recognized the name of someone that he knew quite well. He read the article to himself and a chill rushed through his tall, slender body. The headline read...

Local Resident Loses Her Battle

Inspiring sophomore nurse, and local resident of Clover Springs, Miss Erica Johnston passed away on Sunday evening after a relatively short battle with an unknown illness. The 21-year-old had been admitted to the Clover Springs Hospital on Halloween night, complaining of headaches and depression. Johnston's health worsened and she was transferred to the city for further tests, but died after a seizure in her hospital room. The family said that their daughter contracted some sort of virus that she contracted while caring for the local children in the pediatrics wing at the Clover Springs Hospital. The family denied any further comment. Funeral services will take place at the Clover Springs United Church on Wednesday, March 11th at 1 p.m.

"Jesus Christ," Donald said out loud. Erica was the young nurse who cared for Jakob when he was still in the hospital. Donald looked down at Jakob, who had fallen asleep. *What in the hell is going on? She was too young.* Donald's thoughts were interrupted by a dog barking in the distance. *She was... she was so uncomfortable when she left the house. Something was wrong...even then.*

He looked toward the entrance of the park and knew it was Misty making a racket and causing a scene. He stood up and folded the newspaper, placing it back in the stroller. Donald still winced from the article that he had just read. As he prepared to leave and head home for lunch, a woman came up the path and had his dog, Misty, healing in tow. It reminded him of Barbara, for a gentle second or two, but then it became quite clear.

The woman walked with a limp and, as she got closer to Donald, he saw that she was very thin. Sickly even. She wore a long, candy-striped dress, and a thick wool sweater over top to keep her warm. She wore sandals and her face drooped with wrinkles. Donald was conflicted as to what was more surprising: this mystery woman's commanding and sudden presence, or the fact that she was able to persuade his dog to enter the park with her.

"Excuse me, is this your dog, mister?" The woman spoke with a rasp in her voice. "I know this is your dog. I've seen this dog before. And I've seen you before too."

"Do I know you ma'am? That *is* my dog. How did you get her to come into the park with you?"

"Which question would you like me to answer first, Donald? I can only answer one question at a time."

"How do you know my name? I don't think we've ever met before."

The frail lady thought for a moment while looking at the sky. "Oh yes, you're quite right, Donald. You really never introduced yourself to me. You were in no condition to do that, now were you?"

"What are you talking about? Who are you? You seem awfully familiar, now that I think about it."

The woman started to cough and slowly turned her head, covering her mouth with her hand. She took a step toward the stroller and looked down at the sleeping infant. "And this would be Jakob, am I right?"

Donald nodded. "How do you know that? Listen lady, you're scaring me a little bit."

"There's no need to be scared. I don't blame you for not recognising me. I'm not here to frighten you. I'm here to give you my personal condolences for the loss of your beautiful wife, Barbara. And to give you a warning that I would suggest you and the rest of your family heed without any questions asked."

Donald looked down at his son; he was awake. Once again the child stared up at his father, sending chills through Donald's frame. "Okay then, I'll bite. Here's what has to happen right now. You need to tell me who you are and how you know my family." Misty stayed calm and lay in the trampled, healing grass. "Then I wanna know about this so-called warning that I must heed without any questions. I feel like we're playing a game here mister."

"Well, aren't you the persistent one." The woman's speech quickened in pace. "Alright Donald, there's no need to get snarky. We knew each other in 1979 for a brief time. In your old house." She looked around. "The house that used to sit right here, on this piece of land."

Donald frowned and remained clueless as to what the strange woman was trying to tell him.

"I helped you once, Donald. I helped your entire family, remember? You and Barbara and your three beautiful children. During your family's difficult times in 1979, Donald… Do you remember now?"

"Oh my God." Donald had an epiphany and it all suddenly made sense. "You…you're the woman who cured my family from the spirit of Jimmy Murphy. You're Maria Prescott, aren't you?"

The old and fragile woman shuffled toward the huge stump and leaned against it. "You know, you've always been quite intelligent Donald, but your mind is weak."

Donald thought he would feel offended, but he didn't. "Okay, that's fair. I deserved that. What in the hell has happened to you, Mrs. Prescott? I remember you as… well, as a heavier woman. I mean no disrespect to you, Mrs. Prescott. Please forgive me, but you look much different than I remember."

"So observant too!" Maria became animated, waving her thin arms around. "Well, unfortunately the doctors in the city think that I have some sort of cancer in my bones. I've only been given one or two years to live." She leaned in closer to Donald. "Between you and me, I think it will be closer to three years."

Donald was caught off guard and didn't know the right thing to say to the dying woman. "Well, you would know better than them…I would imagine." He hesitated. "I'm sorry, Mrs. Prescott, I didn't know."

"Of course, you didn't know, Donald. I just told you."

The two stared at each other for a moment. Donald kept looking peripherally at his son to see where his eyes were, but much to his building anxiety, they remained trained on him.

"What is this warning that you need to tell me about, Mrs. Prescott? I need to get back for lunch and you don't want to see the baby when he's hungry, trust me."

Maria stood up straight and shuffled over to the stroller once more. Finally, Jakob changed the direction of his view and looked at the old woman. "Your son is sick. He needs me to help him." She reached down and retrieved the newspaper from the bottom of the stroller, throwing the paper down on the stump table and ensuring that the article about Erica Johnston was in full view. "If you don't let me help you, more people are going to get hurt. More people will die. And I don't imagine that you want that to happen, now do you Donald?"

Donald sat up and snatched his dog's leash from Maria. He looked over to his son and they began to ready themselves for their journey home. A murky and foreboding attitude seeped into Donald's mind.

"Listen, Mrs. Prescott, I'm not interested in anymore of your cruel shenanigans. Every time you're around, bitterness seems to follow. I'm sorry for your condition, but I think we have spent enough time together." With that Donald turned away and they headed down the familiar path and toward the street out front. He had nothing else to say to the old woman and had heard quite enough from her.

"You're making a big mistake, Donald." She tried to raise her voice, but her condition made it difficult. "You will be sorry, Donald. You will be gravely reminded of your poor decisions."

The spring and summer months of 1981 were upon the town of Clover Springs. These would need to be the seasons of restoration for the Sterling family. Donald was well aware that healing would take time. But he also knew that time was never guaranteed…or deserved.

7
Well Now, Isn't That…Strange

February 18, 1982

FOR the first time in many months, everything appeared 'normal' for the Sterlings. Richard was immersed in year two of his studies in the city and was assured a job with a popular engineering firm when he was done school in late May.

Mary remained stoic and mature, while dealing with her mother's loss. Despite a nasty case of the chicken pox around Christmas time, she had happily assumed the responsibility of being one of her little brother's primary caretakers.

Amanda helped out, but lately the ten year old had started secluding herself in her bedroom. Mary was busy with Jakob most of the time, and Donald was out taking photos when he had the clients and the opportunity. He had been a bit detached since the brief conversation with Maria Prescott, and chose to trust his two beautiful and capable daughters with his youngest son's childcare.

Barbara's memorial novel was now published and her literary agent notified Donald of the release. He knew that the story of his family's unfortunate experiences were now available throughout the world, for all to read, but he had no interest in reviewing the final product. It was far too painful.

Donald had started to drink a little bit. He never used to but this was his way of coping with the passing of his wife. The girls were noticing a slight change in his behavior because of it. It was a change in behaviour that hadn't been recognized since the horrific events that took place at the Murphy house. It was a behavior that the girls were petrified of, to say the least. But life for the Sterling's was as good as could be expected.

Jakob had developed into a very unique child. Now nineteen months old, he was walking like any ordinary boy his age, and he was also beginning to form some resemblance of real words with his undeveloped but captivating mind. It wouldn't be long before he would be talking in full sentences, but it was the facial expressions and the noises that came from the little boy's mouth that concerned the family. They were troubling, to say the least. Something was happening to Jakob, as he aged. As his bones grew bigger and his features began to define his boyish looks, the young, yellow-eyed child looked menacing. When his long, black hair was combed back, he would just mess it up. When his face was washed and spotless, he would find the closest grime and resolve that inconvenience. And when his diaper was changed, he found it appealing and considerate to soil it as soon as possible. His clothing was torn and grimy, by choice, and his audible noises were dark and troubled. Jakob was nearing the fabled terrible twos. The family thought, *honestly though, how terrible could they really be?* Jakob was relatively prepared to show everyone, just how very special he really was.

As four in the afternoon neared, the weather outside was absolutely horrid, even for a February. The Sterling family were burrowed into the cosiness of their own home whenever possible. Down in the comfortable, but chilly basement, Donald stretched out on the sofa and watched the football game on television while drinking a scotch on the rocks. It was already his third for the day.

Mary was off to school with a friend, to gain extra credits for a science project that they had been working on, and was due by the next day's afternoon class. She was in her senior year now, and refused to get her driver's license, as her friend was more than happy to be the taxi for her and their other friends.

It had been arranged that Amanda would keep an eye her little brother, and rely on her father should there be any unmanageable issues that she needed to deal with. The youngest daughter embraced the challenge and strove to impress.

"Amanda, hurry up will ya? I have to go. Gloria will be here soon." Mary barked her commands and made Misty cower to the living room where she nestled down beside Jakob's play pen.

"I'm coming." Amanda stomped her feet down the hallway from her bedroom, and met her older sister at the front door. Jakob was wide awake and was playing very aggressively with his toys.

Mary was impatient with her sister. "Listen, he needs to have his bottle in about twenty minutes. Don't forget. He gets pissed when it's not on time, and I'm not gonna cover for you if something happens again. Trust me, Dee-Dee, Dad won't be happy if you screw up."

"I know that," Amanda snapped back. "I'm not feeling very good tonight. I told Dad that I might just call in sick to school tomorrow. I'm probably just going to keep him with me in my room. Dad's downstairs anyway. He'll be fine Mary."

"Okay, just don't screw up Dee-Dee. Dad probably won't be in any shape to jump in and help in a couple of hours." Mary's friend, Gloria, pulled up on the quiet street outside in her mother's car. "Okay, I've got to go. I'll be back by ten." Mary looked over to Jakob as she opened the front door and blew him a kiss. "Bye-bye, Jakob. I love you. You be a good boy for your big sister okay?" She then sprinted out the door and down the sidewalk to catch her ride.

Amanda took a deep breath and then covered up her mouth as she coughed. It seemed as if she was coming down with something.

It was never a good time. She sighed and moved into the living room where Jakob had stopped playing and stood up quietly staring at his older sister. Amanda had developed into a kind and beautiful pre-teen. She knew she was capable of caring for her brother by herself. He had never been a problem for her at any other time. She would show them.

"Come on, Misty, let's go for a sleep in my bedroom." Amanda picked up Jakob, and as she removed him from his webbed cage, he let out a scream and a callous growl that startled Amanda and made her drop the boy onto his feet, where he continued to his butt and then onto his back. Jakob hit his head on the floor and started to cry. Amanda's adrenalin pulsated and this caused great fear, so she reached down to scoop him up swiftly. All she could think of was her father, and the inebriated state that he was in.

Misty had fled the scene when Jakob let out his howl, and was half way down the hallway, cowering in horror. She was getting on in age, now six and a half years old, and hastily became less and less impressed with little Jakob's constant, irritating expressions.

"What's going on up there?" Donald marched up the stairs. "What's the bloody reason for the screaming now?"

"Uh, there's no problem, Dad. Everything's fine. He just fell over and bumped his head, that's all."

Donald staggered over to his son and daughter, clearly showing the effects of his simple cocktails.

"Are you okay, buddy?" His breath was stagnant and revolting. "Do you want me to take him with me downstairs, Dee-Dee?" His words were slurry. "He can watch the football game with me until your sister gets home. What do you think about that?" He looked back to Jakob. "What do you think about that for an idea, champ? Do you want to come and watch the game with the old man, downstairs?"

Jakob made direct eye contact with his drunk father and managed a twisted smile. He then projectile vomited directly onto Donald's chest. The child's concoction of green peas, chicken pieces and grape juice, from his late lunch, ran down his father's body leaving small chunks on the living room floor. Donald retreated with a nauseating expression on his face.

"Oh, that's so gross," Amanda shrieked at her little bother's display. "That's so nasty, Jakob. Wait here Dad, and don't move. I'll get you a towel from the bathroom." She ran down the hallway and giggled at the expense of her father's unlucky misfortune.

Donald looked up from his soiled clothing and back to his son, who stared at him, directly in the eyes, and didn't waiver. "Thanks a lot, boy. That's real nice of you. Why'd you do that?"

Jakob bared his few, newly growing, teeth to his father and uttered a disturbing growl at him. It was fortunate that Amanda had rushed back into the living room and given her father a towel to clean himself up with. The tensions were high, once again.

"Oh, thanks, Dee-Dee. I tell you what. You just go ahead and take him with you then. I need to go and clean this shit up and get back to my game downstairs." Donald looked up at the clock. "It's about time for him to have his bottle anyway, isn't it?"

"Yes, Dad, I'll go and give it to him now. We'll be in my room if you need anything okay?"

"Sure, Dee-Dee, that sounds like a good plan to me."

Donald stumbled away to clean up and wash his hands. It was his priority to get back to the basement, and the football game, where he could indulge in another highball. His direction had shifted and it was disgusting to the children.

Amanda scooped up Jakob and flopped him over her shoulder where she had placed a small towel, in case her brother was not finished getting sick. His mood had seemed to improve now that his father had left, and he didn't seem like he was going to give his sister any further difficulties.

After a short period of time, Amanda sat on her double bed and fed her brother his bottle. He drank it happily and made funny noises, as per usual, as he slurped back the concentrated contents from the glass bottle. The pre-teen turned on her radio and listened to her music until Jakob was content and his stomach's contents had been renewed. With Amanda's help, the little boy lowered himself onto the floor and sat down where he started playing with a large race car toy. He pushed it back and forth and made screeching sounds while crashing it into his own knee on a regular occasion.

As the clock advanced to 5:11 in the afternoon, Jakob suddenly stopped playing with his car. His attention shifted to the corner of Amanda's bedroom and his messy dark hair began to react to electricity in the air. Amanda hadn't noticed yet, but Jakob was fully aware and stared at the source of the energy with an unswerving glare. He slowly got onto all fours and pushed with his hands until he stood straight up. Amanda was rather used to her little brother exploring his environment now that he was fairly comfortable on his own two feet. Jakob walked over to the corner of the room and reached out his right hand toward an invisible force that seemingly commanded the corner of the bedroom and alerted the little boy.

Amanda looked up to check on Jakob and watched him as he stood in the corner of her room, like a punished school mate, less the dunce cap.

"Hey, Jakob, why are you just looking at the corner like that? You can see there's nothing there, right?" She felt that something was there, indeed, but looked for Jakob to agree.

The boy didn't react to Amanda's questioning and stood, like a statue, memorized by the hidden source. The alarmed sister tried to throw her legs over the side of the bed to get up and explore, but they were heavy and unresponsive. *What's happening?* She thought to herself. *I can't move.*

"Jakob! What are you doing?" She had become restless and irritable. "You come here now. Come and see me right now." She tried once again to move her legs, but it was to no avail, and a sense of helplessness creeped into her thoughts.

The young lad started to turn and the electricity in the room became more persistent, and near overwhelming. He finished his turn and pointed his crooked finger at his sister as he slowly fumbled his way forward to the side of the bed. Amanda grabbed at his arm and lowered it away from her face. She could now recognize the flowing current in the room and watched as the hairs on her arm stood at attention. *She didn't even notice her brother's hair... reaching out in all directions.*

At that moment, a brilliant flash of light illuminated the corner of the room and projected it's brightness across the entire space. Jakob didn't even notice, or at least he didn't care to notice. Amanda Sterling could only watch, in sheer anticipation, at the illumination as it began to form into a tall and slender shape. The light flickered on and off for a few seconds and then finally pulsated, one last time, before the brilliant anomaly disappeared into the wall. All went quiet and the imposing power was, all of a sudden, gone. Amanda could move her legs again and jumped out of bed, grabbing her brother and bolting out of the room.

As the frightened children made their way down the hallway, the doorbell rang. It stopped Amanda in her tracks and made her heart skip a beat. Jakob started to growl again as Amanda approached the front door. She first pushed her ear to the door to listen, then her mouth came within an inch of the solid wood divider.

"Who is it?" she asked. It was silent and no one from the other side of the door was courteous enough to offer any type of response.

Amanda looked through the peep hole and saw a woman behind the door, wearing a winter jacket and a scarf that was wrapped around her face. The family's guard dog, Misty, was out in the backyard, and wouldn't provide any security for her at this time. But feeling like she was in no danger, Amanda steadied Jakob with her right arm and opened the front door with her left.

"Yes, can I help you?" she asked with a slight shudder in her voice. Jakob's lip turned downward and he pouted.

"Please, child," the woman on the front steps pleaded. "May I come in? It's awfully chilly outside." Her voice was deep and crackled when she spoke. "It is I, who has come to help you, my dear."

Amanda realized that the elements were cruel and let the woman pass into the house where she closed the heavy door behind her.

She was somehow familiar, but Amanda just couldn't remember, as she had changed so much over the last three years. The mid-height, slender stranger, unwrapped her scarf and smiled at Amanda, still shocked, before directing her attention to Jakob.

"Hello again, my child. I'm afraid that time is getting on and I really don't have much of it left." She looked back to Amanda and a concerned expression crossed her face. "Things will only get worse, my dear. Like they were before. I would strongly suggest that this little one come with me now...Don't you think so? Before it's far too late?"

Amanda was shocked by the sickly woman's words. "What are you talking about? No you can't just take my brother. I think I'd better get my Dad. He's downstairs."

"Wait child!" The woman reached out and grabbed Amanda with her skeletal hand. "Your father already knows, my dear. I've already told him."

Amanda was folding from intimidation, but she could see the disgust on Jakob's face as he looked at the woman so the girl became brave. "I think you should leave...right now. I'm not interested in your 'help' and you're scaring the baby."

After a brief and awkward pause, the stranger looked into Jakob's eyes and submitted. "My time on this Earth has almost expired little one. I will be back for you. Mark my words, I will end the pain and suffering, once and for all. You can count on that little one."

The old woman turned and walked out the door, never looking back. Amanda didn't know what she should worry about more: the energy in bedroom that appeared once again, or the bizarre visitor. She could only imagine what the obviously senile woman meant by her truly distressing warning.

8
Family Reunion

September 4, 1982

So much had transpired over the past seven months, but there was nothing too alarming to report. Donald was still drinking and was barely sober these days. He was able, though, to control most of the frightening outbursts that alcohol tended to cause some people. He just went about his days and was in a relatively good mood most of the time.

Amanda ended up telling Mary about the eccentric woman who came to the house, but it was laughed off and they were both convinced that it was simply an old, and nearly decrepit stranger who had lost her mind. In fact, Amanda was severely reprimanded by her older sister for even letting the stranger into the house. The woman could have been a threat to the safety of both her sister and her little brother. The two girls remained resilient and they would continue to watch out for their brother's wellbeing and care for his needs.

Richard had returned to Clover Springs for the summer. He was a stranger to Jakob, who treated him as such and maybe even worse than his own father, at times. He had graduated from university and started his first full-time job in less than a week. He saw that his father had changed. He was nowhere near the condition he was in at the old house. But Donald seemed to be aging prematurely. The booze was an obvious contributor.

Mary had graduated from high school, and she made sure to mention her mother, in her valedictorian speech, as a solid rock in her upbringing. More than half of the tiny packed gymnasium wept. She decided to take a year off and choose what she was going to do next, whether it be more schooling, like Richard, or perhaps work for a while and gain some experience. Either way, Mary knew that she was still needed at home to help care for her little brother.

Amanda had just started grade six and was eleven years of age now. She hadn't experienced the strange energy in her bedroom lately, but she felt that if she kept things hushed from the rest of the family it would, more than likely, occur again.

Jakob's temper grew as he aged. He made a fuss with his food. He fussed about his toys and his bedtime too. Now completely off his bottled milk, he preferred red meat, cut to his specifications. Most of the other choices of cuisine were usually discarded onto the floor from his metal highchair. He didn't really scream anymore, but continued to growl and made unusual facial expressions, sometimes raising his eyebrows high and revealing his crooked baby teeth. Now, more than two years old, he had become an increasingly greater problem. He really didn't seem to like anybody. He could handle his two sisters, but his father and older brother were nothing more to him than a severely inconvenient nuisance. Jakob was growing fast. He was big and strong for his age, but not overweight and clumsy. With Donald, usually somewhat inebriated, and Richard living in the city, Jakob was beginning to claim the house as his kingdom. The girls were well aware of this, but they had learned that upsetting their little brother was not worth the consequences.

On this late summer day, Donald had just finished eating breakfast and was scheduled to shoot a wedding down in front of the old mine's entrance at the outskirts of town. He was sober, at least, but that was expected by all, as it was only ten in the morning. Richard and his sisters would stay at home today and take turns watching Jakob and keeping him entertained. Maybe some sort of a fun game was in order. It really all depended on the toddler's mood.

Misty was sick. She had been for a few days now, but Donald refused to take his companion to the veterinarian, citing that the dog had probably just got into something outside, and would feel better soon. Poor Misty spent her days lying in the living room, letting the sun from the large picture window shine onto her ailing body.

"Okay I really have to go. These guys are getting married at noon today. It's kind of a strange time for a wedding, don't you think?"

Richard nodded his head. "Well, maybe they want the night to end quicker, that's all. They probably have some sweet action happening later tonight and want a head start, if you know what I mean."

Donald smirked at his son, but his sisters certainly weren't impressed. They circled their brother and gave him grief.

"Oh my God, get a life Rich. Is that all you guys think about? Uh, never mind, I already know what the answer to that question is." Mary lifted her eye brows to the ceiling, but couldn't conceal her less innocent thoughts and cracked an attentive smile.

"You're a sick man, Richard," Amanda added. "Bye Dad, we'll be fine here. Don't worry about us."

Donald grabbed his camera bag off the closet door knob, and headed out to his old red van.

By one in the afternoon, everybody had finished their lunch. Even Misty had some of her chunky kibble, but wasn't looking much better. Jakob was especially fussy on this specific day and having Richard around, certainly didn't seem to enhance the circumstances. It was obvious that Jacob was not fond of his big brother. This affected Richard's fragile perception of himself, as he couldn't understand how such an innocent little boy could have so many wicked feelings for his brother who exuded nothing but love. The three oldest Sterling children cleaned up and carried on a conversation in the kitchen.

"Hey guys, do you want to play a game with Jakob?" Mary, surprisingly, didn't have any plans on this Saturday night, despite meeting a new boy in her senior year. She made it clear to him, at the beginning, that her little brother would need to be her priority for a while; the noble gentleman understood and gave her the space she needed for now.

"What are we going to do?" Richard shrugged his shoulders and scowled, as if playing any type of game would be an inconvenience. "I mean, it's not like he can really do anything yet. He can't catch or throw or even play hide and seek yet."

Amanda decided to throw in her two cents. "Jakob needs to have his nap. Look at the time. I'm surprised he isn't asleep yet." The three of them looked into the room where Jakob was rolling around in his playpen.

"Well, if he's going to sleep, I will too. I'm beat and can use a nap." Richard yawned and covered his mouth.

"Oh, sure Rich." Mary could see right through him. "You go for a sleep and leave us to look after Jakob, like usual. I don't think so buddy."

"Oh, let him go and nap, Mary." Amanda stuck up for her older brother and stood tall in her skin tight blue jeans. "I don't mind watching him, really."

"Do you mean that Dee-Dee? That would be really cool if you wanted to do that. I wouldn't mind going into my room and calling Curtis. I haven't talked to him in a couple of days."

"Ugh, Curtis." Richard rolled his eyes. "Are you going to marry this guy or what Mary?"

Mary reached for an oven mitt from the kitchen counter and threw it at her brother. "No! Geez…Get out of here then and have your nap, but remember, when you and Jakob wake up, he's your responsibility. Got it?"

The three of them all went their separate ways. Richard retreated downstairs into the spare bedroom, where he locked the door behind him. He didn't want any further distractions, but he turned up the volume on his father's stereo system and listened to a mixed cassette tape that he had brought from the city while he attempted to nap. Amanda went into the living room and watched as Jakob grew weary and relocated himself into his customary fetal position to sleep. After only a few minutes Jakob was in never-never land and displayed his familiar growling noise that resonated from his nose and lips.

The lights in the living room flickered and the natural light from the front yard, pierced the inside walls and then retreated, just as quickly. Amanda ensured that Jakob was asleep before walking down to the end of the hallway, where the bathroom was. She locked the door from the inside and sat on the toilet to relieve herself. Once she was finished, she began to wash her hands and was startled by the blazing temperature of the water. She pulled her hand away in pain and quickly turned the hot water faucet off. After regaining her wits, Amanda turned on the cold water that was warm at first touch; gradually it became hotter as she rapidly washed her hands. Amanda stood back and stared at the bathroom sink in confusion. She dried her hands and left the bathroom to tend to her brother, who was sleeping in his playpen. Misty greeted Amanda at the entrance to the living room area. She whined slightly and looked at Amanda with droopy eyes and a bowed head.

"What's the matter girl? Are you feeling any better? Do you want to chew on a new piece of rawhide girl?" Amanda ran to the kitchen and grabbed a new rawhide bone from the cupboard under the sink. "Here you go, Misty. This will make you feel better."

Misty remained mute and lifted her head high for moment, gesturing to Jakob's play pen. She was clearly trying to show the young girl something.

Amanda monitored the dog closely and turned her eyes toward her brother's napping spot. At first, she could see his blue, Sesame Street blanket, and the stuffed teddy bear, that was missing both of its button eyes. She found herself having to side step her pet to proceed into the living room. Amanda was shocked. Jakob was gone! He wasn't in his play pen. Amanda had only been gone for two…three minutes, tops. She scanned the living room and tried to understand how her brother could have escaped the confines of the play pen, but more importantly, where had he gone in such a short period of time? He must be in Mary's room. *That was it.*

Mary must have come out of her bedroom when she was in the bathroom and scooped Jakob up, taking him back with her. Amanda hurried out of the living room, passing Misty, once again, who hadn't moved much and went directly to her big sister's room. She crashed the bedroom door open and startled Mary, who was immersed in a steamy and promiscuous conversation with her boyfriend, Curtis. She threw the receiver down on the bed and scolded her little sister.

"What are you doing, Dee-Dee? What happened to knocking first? Jesus, what's wrong with you?"

Amanda quickly searched the room and didn't see Jakob anywhere. Panic ensued. "Where's Jakob, Mary? Are you guys playing some sort of a cruel joke on me?"

Mary jumped out of her bed and picked up the receiver. "Jesus, Curtis, I have to go! Amanda lost the baby, or something. I'll have to call you back a little later. Yeah…yeah…okay, bye." She ran over to her sister who was frozen at the doorway.

"Why weren't you watching him?" Mary yelled at her sister. "You said you were okay with keeping an eye on him Amanda! Why didn't you tell me that you needed some help with him?"

"I was in the bathroom for a second. He was sleeping, Mary. He couldn't have gotten out of the play pen. He's never done it before. We have to find him. Help me find him, please?"

Mary ran to the empty play pen and started to call out her brother's name. "Jakob? Jakob? Dee-Dee, check in Dad's room. I'll go down and check the basement."

"He can't go down into the basement alon-" Amanda was interrupted.

"Just go!" Mary shrieked again. "I don't have time to argue with you right now! For God's sake, Dee-Dee, just do as I ask, please. Go and check in Dad's room."

Amanda ran down the hallway. She checked her father's bedroom and looked in the bathroom again, but he was nowhere to be seen. Mary came running upstairs.

"He's not down there. Rich is still sleeping. I don't think it's a good idea to wake him up and tell him that you lost Jakob right now, do you? Honestly Dee-Dee, how do these things happen anyway? He's too young to just walk off on his own. What are we going to do, huh? This is so bad."

Amanda shook her head and Mary's attention shifted to Misty, who was making her way to the back landing where she stared out the back screen door.

"Okay, now Misty needs to go outside." Mary started walking toward the door, thinking of what to do next.

"Mary, Misty can use her doggie door if she wants to go outside. I don't think she wants to go out."

Mary opened the door, but the dog froze and stood her ground before casually looking up to the Sterling's oldest daughter. "What's up girl? Do you want to go out or what?"

Amanda's eyes grew big. "What if she's trying to tell us something? Like Lassie does on TV. What if Jakob crawled out of the doggie door and ran away, somehow? Maybe he will go out on the street and someone won't see him and he might be hit by a car or something." She began to breath heavier than she was before.

Mary understood her sister's scenario and ran outside to see if, somehow, Jakob had made his way outside. After turning 360 degrees, she started to cry and ran back into the house.

"Okay, Amanda, we have to wake Richard up now. He needs to help us. We have to find Jakob! What if someone kidnapped him? What if someone broke into the house and took him from right under our noses?"

The two continued to fret, and they jogged down the basement stairs together, waking up their older brother.

An hour had passed and there was still no sign of Jakob. Richard had called the police, who had come by to hear a statement and get a description. Technically, he needed to be gone for twenty-four hours before he could even be considered missing, but because of his age, they made an immediate correction to the rules. *Surely he would be found*, Richard thought. Clover Springs only had a population of 2,800 people. *Someone would see the child and alert the authorities.* That made the most sense.

The three Sterling children sat on the sofa in the living room and sweated from the early afternoon sun that pounded down on the house. There was no way to notify Donald. All they knew is that he was out near the mine today. A squad car that was on patrol would drive by and let him know.

The front doorbell rang, now nearly two hours since Jakob had went missing. Misty managed a loud bark before laying her head down, once again. Mary jumped up to see who was there, and in her distress, didn't even check the peephole, or ask any pertinent questions. On the other side of the door stood a Clover Spring's police officer, and he was holding little Jakob in his arms.

"Oh, thank God," Mary could breathe again. "There you are J! Where did you find him, officer?"

The cop had a stern look on his face and didn't crack a smile. "We found him down at the cemetery, miss. He was sitting on one of the plots there. The cemetery is more than a mile away from here...any idea how he might have made it there, by himself? I'll tell you what, he didn't want to leave there, that's for sure."

Richard bent down to Jakob's height and scolded his brother. "Jakob, how did you get to that place? What were you doing there? How...?"

Jakob slowly lifted his head and his yellow eyes pierced into Richard. He started to growl at his brother, and once again, bared his teeth.

"Uh...it's okay officer. We'll look after him from here. I'm sorry that you had to get involved. It sure won't happen again, I promise you." Mary was embarrassed and wasn't sure how she was going to explain this to her father.

"Well, you understand that we have to report this to your dad. He's gonna want to know what happened. And, come to think of it, the more I try and figure this out, the more I need to know what happened too."

Mary stepped forward and picked up Jakob, holding him close to her chest. "Believe me, officer, I'll make sure that this doesn't happen again. We are all surprised that he would be that mobile so suddenly." She turned and looked at Amanda with a stern look in her eyes.

The middle-aged police officer reached up and removed his hat. "Here's the thing I don't understand. Jakob, there was all alone, sitting on one of the grave plots." He raised his eyes to Richard. "Didn't you folks used to live in the old Murphy house on the other end of town at one time?"

"Uh, yes we did. For a few years anyway. Why?" The oldest sibling questioned the relevance of the officer's off beat remarks.

"Well," the cop seemed considerably bewildered, "Uh, well you see…here's the thing…little Jakob here just so happened to be sitting on the grave of one of the Murphy family." He put his hat back on his head and looked at all four Sterlings. "There's four hundred souls resting there. Now, I'm no Sherlock Homes, but that seems to be a bit of a strange coincidence, don't you think?"

9
Motherly Instinct

May 7, 1983

DISTANCE was gradually pulling the Sterling family apart. The distance of Richard working fulltime in the city. The distance of Donald drowning his anxieties away with a concoction of different scotches. It was the odd distance of Jakob, and the fear that he was only getting worse. His behavior deteriorated, now in his third year. He mumbled his expressions, like a deaf boy who heard too well. No English words had passed his lips and even the partially dependant father, was noticing and dropping hints to the girls to come up with a solution. His efforts would continually fall short with his Jakob.

Mary had been spending more 'special' time with her boyfriend, Curtis, and was about to turn eighteen. She was even spending nights at his place. Most of the time though, Donald wasn't even aware, as he was passed out on the sofa, or he was working in his customized dark room, that he had built, beside the laundry appliances.

Amanda had gradually transformed into the primary care taker. She kept a razor-sharp eye on her little brother, ever since the bizarre mishap, eight months ago, that still had the whole family puzzled.

But Jakob hadn't tried that stunt again. He was fully mobile, but secure locks were installed on the doors, and Misty's doggie door had to be all closed up.

Misty had conquered whatever was effecting her health awhile back. She was slowing down, but she was still an intricate part of the family, and even Jakob had begun to stroke his retriever on occasion. Misty didn't seem to mind, but always remained cautious of the little boy's touch.

As daylight surrendered into the night's full moon, Amanda slowly made her way down into the basement, carrying Jakob in her arms. Donald had, once again, passed out on the couch, but Amanda needed his opinion. She was graduating from her elementary school in a couple of weeks and wanted to model the dress that Donald had bought for her, just last week. Mary was away with Curtis, and Richard was in the city working. She wanted an opinion and her need to be recognized as beautiful was calling out to her. With her engagement to Jakob's needs, her outside friendships were rare. Her father, despite his condition, was still her rock.

"Dad, wake up." She gently nudged Donald with her left arm. Jakob began to fidget and growled sharply. "Dad, please, wake up. I wanna show you something."

Donald stirred and moaned as he woke up. He looked at his son and daughter through squinted eyes and let out a silent burp. "What's the matter now, Dee-Dee? Is everything okay?" He sat up from his horizontal position and covered his face with his hands.

"Dad, what do you think?" Amanda developed a huge smile and started to wiggle her hips in her teal green, ankle-length dress.

Donald stood up, took a quick glance at his daughter and stumbled toward the staircase to the main floor. "It's really great, honey. You're going to be the belle of the ball." He started laughing at, what he presumed, was a funny joke, and continued up the stairs where he went into the master bedroom and slammed the door behind him.

Amanda was so disappointed by her father's reaction and lack of appreciation. She bent down and placed Jakob on the carpet and he immediately commenced with an exploration of the basement, starting with Richard's room. Amanda missed her mom a great deal, now more than ever. She felt all alone. It still hurt and, without even knowing it, the entire family was affected in one way or another. Time had not yet healed all the wounds and young Amanda could only cope the best way she knew how to.

Jakob came out of the spare bedroom and stood about twelve feet from his big sister. Amanda looked over and noticed him, but he was acting more peculiar than usual.

"Jakob? Are you okay? Did you go poopy? It's time for bed anyway. You must be tired huh?" She walked toward her brother and the sequence from her dresses collar shone on the white drywall. As she got closer, Jakob slowly backed into the bedroom, keeping his eyes on Amanda the whole time. "What are you doing? How come you're acting so strange?"

As she entered the bedroom, Jakob had completely turned around and pointed to the unmade bed. He didn't move and Amanda could see, quite clearly that the bed was vacant. Then she turned her head quickly toward the light switch in the room. *How did that get turned on?* She thought. Her eyes went back to Jakob and as she was about to speak, her little brother started to hum. It was shallow and unrecognizable to Amanda, but she just assumed it sounded, somewhat, like a lullaby. The hairs on her arms stood up and she felt the overwhelming, familiar, electrical sensation again.

"Uh...Jakob? What are you doing? What are you doing?" she kept repeating. "You're really scaring me J. Whatever you're doing, please stop."

The bed started to vibrate and its legs scribbled on the bedroom's hard wood floor. Amanda's nose could smell an unusual odor, and it reminded her of burning toast, but much, much less appetizing. All at once, the bed's mattress began to glow and Jakob's eyes grew to the size of silver dollars. Amanda shuddered and felt that this time, things were different. This time, she was quickly reminded of the experiences in the old house.

The bright light intensified and both Amanda and Jakob were forced to cover their eyes. Instinctively, Amanda rushed to pick up her brother and as she did, a fascinating sight appeared. The light dulled to a bearable luminosity. It was a tall, and slender woman. She appeared beautiful, but her facial features were difficult to make out. She wore a long, white nightgown and held an infant in her arms, covered in a colourless blanket. Her body was translucent and her legs faded to non-existence below the thighs. The amazing specter had a neutral expression on her face and her long, blonde hair flowed behind her, like it was being blown by a breeze. She hovered above the ground while Amanda and Jakob looked up at her in astonishment. Amanda shook, but Jakob remained relatively calm in light of the bizarre circumstances. The girl's mouth hung open and she put her brother down, once again.

"Who...who are you?" Amanda found the strength to ask the nearly disembodied spirit. "Why are you here?"

The shining anomaly gently closed her eyes and her mouth shut tightly. After a moment, she stared down at Jakob, and Amanda showed signs of going into shock. She couldn't believe her eyes and she contemplated whether she should run upstairs to get her father or not. But before she could make her final decision, Jakob leisurely turned himself around to address his terrified sister. He wiped his nose on his bare forearm and let out a feeble giggle.

As Jakob opened his mouth, he made the motions to speak for the first time, but as a slight sound began to pass through his lips, a familiar voice cut through the thick basement air and stopped him.

"Amanda? Are you down here? Do you have Jakob? I kind of got this weird feeling that you were down here. I need to talk to you, Dee-Dee."

Mary's high pitched voice disrupted the phenomenal aura and the delightful and spectacular ghost of the floating woman with a young child crackled and disappeared into thin air. Mary ran into the room with mascara streaking down her face. She reeked of marijuana and needed a shoulder.

"You are down here." Clearly distressed, Mary started to cry. What are you guys doing?"

Jakob payed no attention to his upset, oldest sister and continued to stare into the back of Amanda's head.

Amanda ran to her distraught sister and gave her a hug. "What's the matter, Mary? You never cry. What happened to you tonight?"

Mary sniffled and confessed her exact reason for her sadness. "Curtis broke up with me. He told me to have sex with him and I said no because he didn't have a condom. I wasn't feeling very good anyway. He just up and dumped me because I didn't put out. Boys are scum Amanda. You're better to steer clear of them."

Amanda was shocked to hear her sister admit that she was in a sexual relationship. She was too naïve to figure it out herself. She increased her pressure on her sister and hugged her even tighter.

"It's okay, Mary. He wasn't worth it anyway. There's lots of boys that are going to want to be your boyfriend."

Mary rubbed her eyes and sniffled again. "Thanks, Dee-Dee. That means a lot to me." She managed a giggle. "But I'm not looking for boys anymore. I'm looking for a good man. A man like Daddy." She thought quickly about her father's addiction. "Well, almost like Daddy." She sighed and changed the topic. "You still haven't answered me. Why are you guys in the empty bedroom downstairs? Isn't it Jakob's bedtime yet?" She looked down at the boy and his eyes didn't move. "Jakob, what are you looking at? What's the matter with him sis?"

Amanda tried to think quickly, but couldn't resist telling the truth. "Mary, There's something that you need to know. I know you won't think I'm crazy."

"What is it, Dee-Dee?" Are you okay? You look like you've seen *another* ghost."

"I've seen something. More than once too. I've never told anyone because you guys are never around, it seems. I haven't even told my friends at school. I shouldn't tell you though because it doesn't feel right and I'm scared."

"Tell me, Dee-Dee. You can tell me anything, you know that. I'm your big sister. Haven't I always had your back? I'll help you, whatever you need. If there's something that you want to tell me about Jakob, go ahead, don't be frightened." Mary held her breath.

Before she could respond, little Jakob tugged on her pant leg. The two girls looked down at their three year old brother who remained fixated on Amanda's face.

"Mummy," Jakob said.

"Oh my God!" Mary exclaimed. "He said Mummy. Did you here that Dee-Dee? He said his first word."

Amanda was astonished and smiled brightly. "Yay, Jakob said his first word. I'm sorry J, but I'm not your mommy. I'm your sister, Dee-Dee. Can you say Dee-Dee? And Mary too…can you say Mary like a big boy Jakob?"

Jakob slowly turned and let out a faint growl. He lifted his right arm and pointed his crooked index finger at the slightly shabby mattress.

"Mummy," he repeated, this time even louder than before. And then he turned his head toward the girls and his bright yellow irises glowed like two identical twin stars. "Mummy!"

10
The Gift That Never Stops Giving

January 3, 1984

A new year had begun and Jakob, now three and a half years old, hadn't spoken a word ever since the unusual experience, down in the basement. By this point, he was a step behind with his vocal abilities. Amanda hadn't see the ghostly woman again, since the spooky experience with Jakob in the basement. Even after the occasional prodding from Mary, she decided to deny anyone the creepy information. It was all she could think about lately though.

The festivities of Christmas and New Year's Eve had passed and even Donald was joining in with his family. Something pulled him near during the important family celebrations. It made him feel closer to Barbara. But he still carried a rocks glass of scotch most of the time. It was a fixture to his arm and you could hear his ice clinking from across the house. His social life was non-existent and his career was a mess, but he stayed relevant to his family and that gave him a certain amount of motivation.

The Gift That Never Stops Giving

Richard was home for the holidays, but missed out spending Christmas day with the family because of a work project that needed to meet a strict deadline. He sat in the downstairs bedroom and packed, ready to make the two-hour drive back to the city in the morning. He was aware that he was reasonably fortunate, as his job allowed him to take week long holidays, at least twice a year.

Mary came down the stairs with Jakob in tow. He was holding his new football tight. It was a gift from an anonymous 'Santa,' who had sent the wrapped ball to the Sterling's address with a plainly written tag that said 'Jakob.' Mary, Amanda, and Richard all convinced one another that their father sent the gift through the mail to impress his young son, but Donald categorically denied it. Jakob hadn't put the football down since it arrived on Christmas Eve. He even insisted that he sleep with it and made it very clear that taking it away was not a very clever option.

Once Jakob saw Richard sitting on the bed, he ripped his arm away from his older sister and took his football into the main rumpus room where he sat and played.

"Hey, Rich, I can't believe you're heading back already. It seems like you just got here, huh?"

"Yeah, well, duty calls I guess. I just want this headache to go away. I've had it almost the whole time I've been here. And come to think of it, I had a bit of a headache the last time I was here too."

Mary lowered her brows and made a pouty look on her face. "Well that's no good. Maybe there's something wrong down here in the basement."

"You mean like mold or something?"

"Maybe, who knows? Why don't you ask Dad?"

The mention of their father allowed Richard to recollect. "Oh yeah, I almost forgot." He reached onto the bed and picked up a newspaper article that he had cut out of the city's local rag. "Look at this." Mary took the paper from him and read as Richard continued. "See that? Front page. Do you remember her, Mary? It wasn't that long ago."

She looked over the article for a moment. "I recognize the name, but the photo isn't her is it?" Mary was suddenly intrigued.

"Oh yeah, that's her alright. That's the very same Maria Prescott that we know. The same woman that saved us from the Murphys."

"Oh, my God," Mary displayed saddened emotions of hopelessness and empathy for the old acquaintance. "She actually died. She succumb to her cancer, it says here. I can't believe she looked so thin…so sickly. What a shame, don't you think, Rich? We have to tell Dad about this, for sure."

"Yes, that's why I brought it. It was in my bag, and I forgot about it until now. I just don't know if he'll even remember her. He was pretty out of it the last time they were in the same room together. Maybe he will, I don't know. Maybe he won't remember just because he's never sober anymore. I'm worried about Dad, Mary. How do you and Dee-Dee deal with it when I'm not here? How do you stop yourselves from just walking away sometimes?"

"It's not easy, Rich. And it seems to get worse each day. He's not violent when he's drunk though, that's a good thing. It's because he can't let go of Mom." She thought about her accusation. "Well, none of us can, I suppose, but Dad is handling it differently than everybody else." She glanced out the rumpus room and could see Jakob on the floor, rolling on his back and making incoherent mumbling sounds. His football stayed within arm's reach.

Richard zipped up his black duffel bag and stood up from the bed where he put his arm around his sister. "You just remember that you have a big brother who's always here for you, okay?"

Mary smiled, nodded, and gave her brother a tender hug before the two of them headed out of the bedroom.

Mary grabbed Richard by the arm and admitted a concern. "Richard, wait a second okay? I need to tell you something."

"Sure, Mary, you can tell me anything. What is it?"

Mary looked over to Jakob and then back to her big brother. "Rich, something is very strange with Jakob."

"What do you mean?"

"Well, it's not just Jakob. Amanda has been acting funny lately too."

Richard bit his lip and shook his head slightly. "Really? I haven't noticed anything weird with Dee-Dee, but Jakob has always been a little…how should I say? Challenging?"

Mary looked back to the bedroom. "I came home about seven months ago and found them both down here in the bedroom, and they were acting very strange. Amanda was going to tell me something, but she never did. Jakob said 'Mummy' and it distracted her."

"Let me talk to her okay?" Richard provided his sister with some reassurance. "I'll get something out of her tonight. She'll tell me if I ask."

After the girls had finished making a lavish pork and roasted potatoes supper with a healthy garden salad, the entire family sat down at the dining room table, to have one final meal together before Richard's return to the city.

Mary placed Jakob on to his booster seat, as per usual, and he ensured that his football was with him. He managed to place it on his lap, below the table top, so he had room to eat his food. Donald had partaken in the liquor a bit too much this evening and stumbled to the table, making a distracting racket on his way. Before taking his seat, he scanned his four children and smiled.

"Well, isn't this nice," he said. "We're all sitting here together as a happy family." He looked to the spot where Barbara used to sit. "Well, we're almost together as a happy family anyway, right?"

"Dad, let's just have a nice meal together okay? We all miss Mom." Mary wasn't afraid to challenge her father's attitude. "Why don't you stop thinking that you're the only one who's suffering, cause' you're not, okay?"

Donald took offense to Mary's tone and snapped back at her. "Listen, you! Did I ask for your God damn opinion? No…I don't think I did, so shut the hell up. Not everything is about you all the time."

Mary was taken aback by Donald's words and sat silently in shock. *You're the biggest concern of all,* Mary thought. He hadn't demonstrated this type of brashness in years...*since...*

Richard passed the peas to one of his sisters and tried to break the uncomfortable vibe around the table. "Dad, I was just telling Mary about that woman who helped us in the old house, Maria Prescott."

Donald lifted his eyes to his son and scowled. "Yeah okay, what about her?"

"She died a couple of weeks ago, from cancer. She was a celebrity in the city. Made the front page and everything."

Donald cut his potato with a sharp steak knife and used enough pressure to create an irritating squeaking on the plate. "Well, it's for the best probably. She was skin and bones anyway."

Richard tilted his head and squinted at his father. "What do you mean? How do you know that? She was absolutely humungous when she was at the old house, don't you remember?"

"Well, if she died from this...cancer, she was probably skinny... Right?" He changed the subject quickly, looking over to his other son. "Okay, Jakob, we're not going to have that ball at the table anymore when we eat." He got up and started to move toward Jakob.

The youngest Sterling child watched intently as Donald neared, and inhaled deeply before letting out a horrific scream, something the family hadn't heard in many months from the growing child. The intensity of the boy's vocal chords shook the kitchen and had the Sterling clan all covering their ears in fright.

"You just never mind and give me that damn ball. You don't need that right now." He reached down to grab the football from between Jakob's legs.

"No," Jakob screamed at Donald. "No, no, no, no!"

Donald fought with his wiggling son to win the fight for the ball. "Well, well, well," he looked around the table. "The boy just said his first words, what do you know?"

Of course, Amanda and Mary knew that this wasn't the case, at all.

The Gift That Never Stops Giving

"Give me that fucking ball, boy." He yanked the ball from his son and tossed it into the kitchen. It was still within Jakob's sight and that seemed to fuel his fire more than before.

Jakob literally freaked out, screaming and shaking his booster seat and rocking the chair to an almost tipping stage. He hissed and growled, yelling at Donald with pure hatred in his voice.

"No! No! No!" he continued. Tears cascaded down his cheeks. His face turned beet red and veins started to pop out on his forehead. He wiggled his seat belt and tried to escape to retrieve his prized football.

Richard stood up and tried to calm the tide. "Why don't you just let him have his ball, Dad? Then he'll quiet down and we can eat in peace."

"Hell no," Donald was fierce. "Maybe he shouldn't even have it after supper if he's going to act like this." He bent down and got right in his son's face. "Do you think you're the only one who can make an ass out of himself?" Donald was clearly inebriated and stuck his pointed finger into Jakob's face. The child screamed even louder and even Misty ran out and into the living room to get away from the irritating squelching.

"Foootballl," Jakob wailed. "Foootballl." He grabbed Donald's finger with his little hand and pointed over at the ball in the middle of the kitchen floor with his other finger. He began to wheeze and attracted everyone's attention. Somehow Richard felt that the situation was not going to turn out well.

Donald laughed. "You can beg all you want kid. You're not getting that ball back until you finish your supper." He let the child squeeze his finger and tempted Jakob to take further action.

Jakob's eyes shone yellow, and he looked down at Donald's obstructing finger with a malevolent look in his eyes. The next moments were inevitable.

Amanda realized what was coming and tried to warn her dad, but she wasn't quick enough. "Watch it, Dad, he's got a full set of teeth and he's going to bi-"

The youngster bit down hard on Donald's finger and the sloshed father let out a scream of his own, yanking his hand away from his son's jaws.

"Son of a bitch!" He raised his arm to smack down on Jakob, but Mary yelled out and stopped him before he could act. "Jesus Christ, boy." He put his finger in his mouth and sucked on it to relieve the pain as he walked down the hall to the washroom, while mumbling a constant line of obscenities to himself.

Amanda stood up from her chair and went to Jakob's side. "Holy crap, Jakob, you shouldn't do that to Daddy. He's in a really bad mood right now. You can have your football back, after you're done your supper, okay?"

Jakob continued to breathe heavy and a slight growl passed his lips, like he was an injured, wild animal. He made fists with his hands and placed them on the supper table.

"No Daddy." He spoke clearly. "Foootballl!"

11
Can You Keep A Secret?

July 28, 1984

JAKOB was four years old and had grown to the size of the average five year old already. His vocabulary had increased substantially, and he was starting to use it more often. The other members of the family were delighted at how their new brother, and son had embraced his new abilities, but the family was now quite cautious of his temper and freedom of expression.

Mary had found herself a part-time job, waitressing, down at the old diner on Third Street. Now, nineteen years old, she wanted some income for herself and didn't want to rely on her mother's life insurance payout to cope. Not that her father would notice. He was a wreck, and was in need of some outside assistance, just like before. This time Donald was possessed by a completely different kind of demon. The kind of demon that was even harder to defeat. He became a shell of his former self, and spent most of his time downstairs watching the television, and drinking. It was Mary, with her newly acquired driver's license, who would make the trips to the liquor store to refill her father's weekly supply of scotch.

Even though it was a Saturday, Mary was forced to work. Richard was in the city and, once again, it was Amanda tending to her younger brother, who had developed into more than a handful. Jakob, Amanda, and Misty all sat in the living room of their small and cozy house and it was nearing three o'clock in the afternoon. Jakob held on to his football, and was still not willing to part with it. He sat on the floor and reached over to stroke his dog, but as he did, he squeezed his hand together, in a fist, and pulled hard on the Golden Retriever's hair. Misty let out a yelp and quickly stood up, where she moved away three feet and lowered her head toward Jakob.

"That wasn't very nice, Jakob," Amanda said. "Why did you do that to Misty?"

"Bad doggie." Jakob said with conviction. "Bad, bad doggie, Misty."

"And why is Misty so bad, J? She didn't do anything to you. How would you like it if someone did that to you?" Amanda reached over to grab at Jakob's long, messy hair to teach him a lesson, but Jakob moved away and used his arm to shield Amanda's progress, letting out a slight growl.

"Okay fine. Well, just don't do that to Misty anymore or she won't like you, do you understand?"

Amanda walked to the large picture window, and stared out into the front yard. The sun was beating down, but there were a couple of dark and ominous clouds in the sky. Donald had announced, earlier in the morning, that the newspaper was calling for thunder showers, a little later in the afternoon.

"Let's go outside and play. What do you think about that J?" She walked over to her brother, who had calmed a bit, and reached out her hand. "Come on, let's go. It will be good for you. We can all go to the backyard." She looked at Misty. "Do you want to come outside, girl?"

Misty stood high and her tail shook, back and forth.

Amanda took Jakob's hand and made her way to the back door. On her way she stopped by the staircase to the basement, and notified her father.

"Dad? We're going out to the backyard, in case you were wondering where we were. I don't think we'll be out there long. It' so hot out there today."

"Take your brother with you!" Donald yelled back at his precious daughter.

"I am. We're just going to play for a while, and then I will start getting supper ready, okay?"

Donald stumbled to the bottom of the staircase and looked up to Amanda. "You be careful out there. Keep an eye on Jakob. I mean it." He pointed his arm at Amanda and it had his rocks glass attached to the end of it. The ice cubes were melting. A good sign that he was ready for another.

Amanda was in no mood to argue. "Okay, Dad, I'll keep an eye on him, don't you worry." Misty was afraid of Donald's demeanor and changed her mind, running up through the kitchen and into the living room where she jumped up on the sofa to take a nap. It was unusual for her to stay away from a chance to play.

Once outside in the backyard, Amanda let go of Jakob's hand and he ran to the other end of the lawn, trying to get Jakob to chase her. But he was not interested in playing with his sister. He was content, just standing where Amanda left him, and twirling his football around in his arms. Jakob stood, three-foot-six inches and wore some torn jeans and a filthy white T-shirt. His hair was all over the place and, despite Amanda's best efforts, his face was an absolute mess. He stared blankly toward his sister and showed little appreciation for her or the hot summer day.

"Come on J!" Amanda begged her brother to engage, but he didn't move. "Oh, you're a lot of fun." Amanda started to walk slowly back to Jakob, and it was then, that he turned and waddled over toward the shed in the front corner of the yard.

Amanda watched as he stood in front of the tiny metal structure and tilted his head in confusion. She instantly clutched her chest and became short of breath at the sight of her brother standing in front of the shed. It reminded her of herself, in the old house, standing in front of her bedroom closet doors, and awaiting her paranormal friend, Dortie, to come on out and visit. Amanda wiped her brow from the perspiration, building up on her teenage forehead and inched closer to the entranced little boy, using caution with each step.

"Jakob? What are you doing? There's nothing in there except bicycles, rakes, and garden gnomes. Why are you staring at the shed anyway? You're scaring me, Jakob. Let's go back inside the house and do something else, huh?" *The heat was becoming a critical factor to how long they would last outside.*

The longer Jakob stood still and stared at the shed's doors, the more terrified Amanda became. *I need some water soon or I'm going to collapse from shock and dehydration,* she thought. She then moved to Jakob's position and snatched him up around the waist, making him let go of his treasured football. He released a tremendous squeal, kicking and flailing as Amanda managed to carry him, back inside.

Once in the landing, Donald was seen, standing at the entrance to the kitchen and he scowled as the kids came in. He wanted to know what was for lunch and he didn't seem to demonstrate much patience.

"Oh shit, here we go again. What in the hell is going on Amanda?" He was not trilled, to say the least. "Every time you're looking after that kid, something happens to him. What's the story this time? Did he bite you?"

"No, he's okay. He didn't bite me, Dad. It's just a weird phase, I guess." Amanda put Jakob down and he squirmed away, around the corner and toward the back door. "Wait, Jakob, I need some water. I'll be there in a minute." She went to the kitchen sink and filled a glass with water as Donald stayed close to her heels and continued to push and ridicule Amanda for a crime she didn't commit.

"Jesus, Dee-Dee, Why can't you keep that kid in better control? It's no wonder he's such an 'A' hole to everyone. You just let him do whatever he wants and never discipline the kid. That's not the way that me and your mother raised you, is it?" His lecture became a rant, and Amanda saw something that scarred her from the past. "Your mother never let you kids walk all over her." It was obvious that Amanda was becoming offended and anger began to creep in to her loving soul, for the first time in a long time. *What do you mean...I never discipline the kid? Isn't that your job?*

"I have an idea." Amanda sipped her water. "How about you try and be there a little bit for him? You're his daddy, aren't you? Maybe you could look after him for a little while instead of drowning your sorrows in that dumb bottle of scotch...What do you think about that?"

Donald was stunned. He stood, and was shaken by his youngest daughter's courage and fortitude. This was short lived though as the intensity of the situation, and the booze in his system, made Donald strike out, smacking Amanda hard in the face, and jolting her sideways, causing her water glass to slip out of her hand and shatter onto the floor.

He was immediately regretful, and he instinctively reached out to console her. "I'm so sorry, honey. I didn't mean it. Really, I'm sorry. I don't know what just came over me."

Amanda cried and held her face in the palm of her hand. She reacted, the only way that she knew how, and bolted out of the kitchen and toward the back door.

It was then that she remembered Jakob. *Where was he?* She panicked. He had come this way, so he had to be in the basement or perhaps outside, having escaped through the back door again. Donald continued to request some forgiveness, but the embarrassed and traumatised teenager was not interested in his words. Her only concern was her brother so she took her chances and bolted toward the back landing, heading outside, remembering that Jakob's football was still out there. She pushed open the door and looked to the shed where she saw her brother, once more.

This time, though, Jakob wasn't in front of the shed doors. He was sitting on the ground beside the far side of the shed. He was fully engaged and had a lively and fully refreshing smile on his face. It was his disturbing actions, though, that stopped Amanda in her tracks and made her short of breath.

The back side of the shed was hidden to Amanda, but Jakob sat within her perfect sightline. Amanda watched intently, and witnessed Jakob's football roll to his knee from behind the shed. He then picked it up and rolled it back. Amanda held her breath as she fearfully waited for the inevitable, and sure enough, the football re-appeared, wobbling back and forth, before gently bumping against Jakob's little running shoe this time. He giggled in delight and continued the game, rolling the ball back to the unseen presence. *Jakob has a friend?* Amanda wondered. The boy was fixated on his guest and completely ignored his sister's presence.

Amanda felt as if her feet were encased in cement, but made it a priority to proceed to a better vantage point. When she made it to Jakob's back and was enlightened by his vantage point, she saw as the ball rolled back to her little brother, Amanda looked up and saw what she expected all along. It was the brilliant apparition of the woman again. She was near translucent and washed out by the sun, but she was most definitely hovering above the ground and interacting with the little boy. Jakob leisurely turned around to look at his petrified sister, and spoke slowly and clearly.

"Mummy. Mummy say shhhh." He lifted his finger to his lips. "Mummy say Jakob is bad. Bad Jakob, Mummy say you can't tell the man. Mummy say shhhh." He then lifted both of his hands high and wiggled his fingers, bending them up and down until he hid both thumbs and his right index digit. He proudly displayed seven fingers and Amanda was impressed that he seemed to know exactly what he was doing.

"What do you mean J?" What do you mean I can't tell the man? Tell the man what?" She looked up to the energy, still glowing about eight feet away. "Who is it, Jakob? Who is the bright light? What does seven fingers mean?"

Jakob stood up and took a step toward Amanda. "Mummy, Amanda, Mummy." He pointed at the ghost.

Amanda was astonished and stared at the glowing spirit while squinting her eyes. Her hopes that the energy was a representation of her mother was intriguing, but extremely intimidating, to say the least.

Suddenly, the bright luminosity disappeared once more as the interaction was interrupted again.

"Dee-Dee, are you guys out here?" Mary had arrived home from work and ran into her father who explained that he and Amanda had just had a pretty serious disagreement.

She turned and saw her two siblings, who were standing in an awkward and confusing state. "What's going on out here? Are you guys alright?" She looked down at her brother. "Jakob, buddy, are you okay?"

Jakob looked up to Mary and opened his mouth. "When Daddy dies, I promise not to eat his bones."

Mary trembled. Her breathing suddenly became shallow and she struggled to ask her four-year-old brother what he could have possibly meant by his terrifying statement.

12
Man's Best Friend

November 13, 1984

ONLY twelve weeks had passed since Jakob displayed his bizarre behaviours in the backyard. This was a turning point for the family. Something was seriously wrong, and now the entire family was on full alert. They were recognising the clarity of the situation and needed to take some action.

Amanda had an apparent secret that she wouldn't share, and neither did Jakob. It was if they had been sworn to confidentiality by the fascinating energy that appeared every once in a while, but not enough to cause anyone any immediate fright. Amanda had speculated about Jakob, showing his seven fingers and had even seen him do it four times since then. She needed to know if the vision was that of her mother and feared that she would never find out if she told anyone. She said not to tell him? Who was 'him' anyway? It didn't matter. Amanda held on to it, tight to her heart.

Mary was an intelligent woman now, who knew that something was unusual with her young brother, but she could not make presumptions. She, as per usual, attempted to keep the peace in the family and carry on with her life, as optimistically as possible.

Richard was extremely concerned. So much so, that he asked for a leave of absence from his job. He wanted to come back to Clover Springs and try to re-attach his frayed and tangled family. His brother didn't like him too much. There was no sense asking him why though. He didn't have an accurate answer. All he knew is that Jakob wasn't his biggest fan and he appeared to be a threat to the boy.

Even Donald was trying to make a better effort. He was well aware that his drinking had become a big problem. He had struck his daughter. He had yelled and even cursed out loud at his *innocent* toddler son. And he had finally surrendered to the luckless fact that he had gradually become a 'distant and unseen' parent to the newest addition of the family. After a lengthy conversation with Richard, Donald swore to cut down on his alcohol intake, but it wouldn't be easy. It was far too tempting to surrender to it. But he would try… *it was all in the mind, right?*

Jakob was quickly developing into a reason for great concern. The family had talked about taking him to the doctor and even checking with a therapist. He was mean, and he lacked a basic conscience, it seemed. He was downright disrespectful and non-appreciative. Jakob was nearing his kindergarten year, and although he was an intelligent little boy, the Sterling family didn't feel that he was socially ready to interact with the general public. He had never had a friend and was kept close to home for the past four years. The family sheltered him to avoid him from being ridiculed for his actions. He wouldn't even know how he was supposed to act in front of strangers. No one ever showed him. *Keep him fed and watered. Make sure he has toys and can play. Give the kid a soft place to lay his head.* That's all that mattered to the two Sterling girls who cared for him the most. *But he needed to start somewhere and maybe he would eventually grow out of his early childhood challenges and adversities,* the family thought. But then again…maybe not.

The AM news station, on their old transistor radio, had announced a record cold snap for the little town of Clover Springs and the entire surrounding county. The six schools in town had shut down for the day, so it appeared that Amanda had an unexpected day off.

As the dependable gas furnace in the basement worked overtime to heat the Sterling's home. Richard was out. His 1982, baby blue, Chevrolet was in need of a tune-up and an oil change, as it was now being shared by his dad and his sister. If the van wasn't available, Richard's wheels were available for all. Upon his return, from a service station, he entered the back door and placed an extra bottle of anti-freeze on the floor, near the family's winter boots.

"Holy cow, there's a lot of snow out there. My little car almost can't make it through this shit." He spoke to his father, drinking a coffee, in the dining room. "Maybe we should only use the van when we need to go out, Dad. Just until the snow gets packed down a little bit. What do you think?"

"Well, with Mary's job and the extra errands, we're kind of used to having both vehicles. But you're probably right, Rich. There's no need for someone to have an unfortunate accident." It was the first intelligent conversation that anyone was able to have with Donald in an awfully long time. He acted like the man he once was, if only for a short period of time.

"I'll put the car on the street later. Then it's there if we need it. It just had a sweet tune-up at the garage anyway."

Misty came running up the stairs from the basement, and sprinted over to Richard, wagging her tail. Grey hairs were evident on her chin.

"Hey, Misty girl. How's my girl doing? You're such a good doggie, aren't you?" Richard's mood was fairly light.

Misty's tongue panted in and out of her mouth. She had been a solid part of the family for eight long years now, and endured all of the same sadness as the rest of the family. Her patience with

Jakob was the most impressive and the aging dog respected and understood the child's need for his own personal space.

"What do you say girl? Should we go get a treat?" Misty dashed to the kitchen and Richard followed while Mary came out of her bedroom and joined Donald at the breakfast table. She wore a colourful outfit and her skin shone from happiness.

"Good morning, Dad. How are you feeling this lovely cold morning?" She gave her father a kiss on the cheek and went to the counter to pour herself a cup of coffee.

"Good morning, sweetheart. I'm feeling okay, I guess. I have a bit of a headache, but after speaking with Rich, last night, I'm not the only one."

"Richard told me that he gets a lot of headaches when he's here. Do you think there's something wrong with the house maybe?"

"Oh, I don't think so, Mary. I guess it's possible, but compared to the last house, I don't really think that there's anything wrong with this house, if you know what I mean. Don't you remember? There were weird sounds and all of those residual spirits. Like the man in the tree, remember?"

An uncomfortable sensation overcame Mary. "Uh, well Dad, I'm not quite sure about this place. I guess maybe you haven't noticed, but there's some strange stuff happening here too. Surely you can feel it."

"Well, sure I do, but I've been afraid of confessing my concerns to you girls, and Richard too. I don't really want to believe that these weird things are still happening to us. How can they still be happening to us, Mary? Haven't we been through enough?"

"I don't know, Dad. All we can do is care for Jakob and be the best support system for him as he gets older. I think it might be a good idea to take him to a professional though. He needs some help, I think. He might be the answer to everything that we're afraid of."

Richard came back into the dining room and joined the other members of his family. He cracked a soda and sat down at the table. "Hey, what are we talking about?"

"We were talking about this house and something strange happening around here. And Jakob, that maybe he needs to go and see a doctor. You agree, don't ya, Rich?"

"Absolutely, I agree one hundred percent. The sooner the better too." He looked around. "Where is the little bugger, anyway?" Richard and Donald shared a laugh together. "I'll go with you because I'd like to know as well."

"Rich!" Mary scolded him. "It's no wonder he doesn't like you guys as much as me and Amanda. Geez, he's in his room, playing Legos with Dee-Dee. Why do you guys think there's something wrong with him?"

"Come on Mary, we're just teasing. Just relax will ya?" Richard defended himself and his father, but Donald only nodded slightly and pushed his glasses closer to his head.

Amanda came out of her room and walked through the kitchen to speak to her family. "Hey guys, Jakob keeps on telling me that he's thirsty. I'm gonna give him some juice, Dad. He keeps saying 'thirsty juice,' 'thirsty juice,' over and over again. It's driving me nuts."

"Bring him out here for some juice, Dee-Dee. Is he in a better mood today?"

"Well, you can see for yourself." She raised her voice and called out to her brother. "Hey, Jakob, come on out to the kitchen and have some apple juice!" Donald felt an immediate intimidation and waited on pins and needles for his son to respond.

Jakob, anticipating a sweet beverage, responded to Amanda's request and exited his room, walking into the kitchen. He paused when he passed the back door landing, where he saw Misty chewing on her new bone, by her food and water dishes. A moment of peace for the little boy was quickly disrupted by an irritating voice and it changed his whole persona, in a heartbeat.

"Hey, buddy, how are you doing today?" Jakob didn't look at his father and ignored his question all together. "Jakob? I'm talking to you son." There was no response. "Look at me boy!" He shouted at the child and he only retreated, moving closer to Amanda.

"Jakob, Daddy is talking to you." Richard tried to get the boy's attention, but as he took a step toward his younger brother, he hissed and swung his arm at Richard.

"Jesus, just forget about it." Donald got up and began storming out of the kitchen. "Somebody talk some sense into that kid before I lose it again. Shit, it's no wonder that I drink." He headed to the basement and Mary ran after him to try and calm him down. She knew that she could possibly be putting herself in danger again, but her father hadn't been drinking today…*yet,* so he should be a bit more reasonable.

Amanda jogged to the refrigerator and poured her brother a cup of apple juice from the kitchen. He instantly removed the scowl off his face and swigged it back in utter delight.

Richard pleaded with Amanda. "Dee-Dee, please tell me what I ever did to piss this kid off so much. I just want him to be my bud, but he hates me for some reason." He looked over, just as Jakob placed his empty cup on the counter. Then, he walked down the four stairs to the back landing to pet Misty. He sat down beside his dog and stroked her golden fur.

"I don't know, Rich. It's with both you and Dad. I don't get it. I can see him being mad at Dad because he hasn't been very nice to him, but you? It makes no sense. It was you and Dad that seemed to get picked on, in the old house too."

"You know that I want to help, but maybe it would just be better if I went back to the city. I don't seem to be doing anything productive here anyway. I know that Jakob won't miss me, that's for sure."

"No, Rich, you can't do that. We need you here. Dad needs you here. He's been good since you moved back home. Don't leave now, please."

He thought briefly. "Okay, Dee-Dee, I won't go. But I'm telling you, we better get Jakob to a doctor before he hurts somebody… or himself. I don't want to be responsible for all of his mistakes."

Jakob returned to his Siblings and tugged at Amanda's pant leg. "Misty is thirsty." He pointed at the dog. "See, Misty thirsty like me…See?"

Amanda turned to look at the family dog, lapping from her water dish. "Yes, Jakob, I can see that. Misty is thirsty, just like you. That's what Misty needs to live. Water, just like Jakob."

"Or juice," Jakob established.

"Yes," Amanda reassured the toddler, "Or juice… yes, that's right."

The three Sterlings moved out of the kitchen and went their separate ways. Amanda took Jakob to the living room and they covered each other in warm blankets on the sofa. Amanda could remember the fireplace in the old house. It was so warm and cozy. Donald remained downstairs and spoke to Mary. He hadn't surrendered to the bottle yet, so she was making some progress with his fragile emotions. Richard went to the washroom to take a shower, and for about an hour, all was quite in the house.

After his shower, Richard went back into the kitchen to see about making some sandwiches for his family. He glanced over to the back door landing and noticed that something was out of place. He walked over to investigate a little closer and became startled. The jug that he had brought home earlier that day, from the automotive shop, had been moved. There was much less liquid in it than when he had come home. He promptly sprinted to the basement where his father was watching television. He was now drinking a tall, unsweetened, iced tea.

"Dad, did you put some of my anti-freeze into the van?" His answer would solidify and orchestrate the next trial and tribulation that the family would be forced to face together.

"No, why? Do you think I need some?" Donald was oblivious to the reasoning for his son's simple question, but Richard felt sick to his stomach, all of a sudden, and his head throbbed like a wrecking ball was active inside. His blood pressure rose and deep concern crossed his face.

Before he could explain, Mary came running down the stairs in a frantic panic. "Dad! Dad!" She cried as she yelled her father's name, and ran into Richard's arms, once at the bottom.

"What's the matter, Mary? What happened? Is Jakob all right? What did he do this time? I can just imagine. Is he okay?"

"Yes, he's sleeping. It's Misty!"

"Misty? What about her?"

"There's something wrong, quick, you have to come and look at her. She's in Dad's bedroom right now and she's sick."

The three of them ran up the stairs and met Amanda in the hallway, as she could hear the commotion. They all made their way to Donald's master bedroom and saw their loyal pet, Misty, laying in a puddle of her own vomit, and convulsing. She was in clear pain and appeared helpless and troubled. Donald had flashbacks of his loyal pet as a puppy.

"Misty, what's wrong girl?" Donald asked as if the Golden Retriever was going to provide him with an intelligent answer.

Richard announced the bad news and had no doubts as to what had happened. "It's the anti-freeze, Dad."

"The anti-freeze?" Mary interjected. "What are you talking about? Where did she get anti-freeze?"

"We don't have time," Richard snapped back. "Dad, help me get Misty to the car. She needs a vet or she's going to die. They'll have to pump her stomach."

Amanda and Mary broke into tears and wrapped their arms around each other. The two Sterling men carried the big dog to the front entrance.

"I'll go and start the car," Richard said. "Wait here for a minute." He through on his boots and downfield jacket. Donald, Amanda, and Mary all stroked their ailing pet and even Donald welled up and released some tears. When he looked at his dog, he couldn't resist seeing his bride, Barbara. She's the one who picked Misty out, at the shelter. They connected immediately and the pain of Barbara's absence was clear again..

"You're okay, Misty. We're going to get you some help, just hang in their girl." Amanda began to wail and she felt as if she was losing her best friend.

After, what seemed to be an eternity, Richard came back into the house, wringing his freezing hands together and breathing heavy.

"I can't start the car. I just got a God damn tune-up. Why won't it start? I need your keys, Dad. We have to get my car out of the way and take the van. I need your help to push my car back and I need your keys."

Donald ran to his bedroom and to the dresser, where he kept his keys, but they weren't there. He looked around the room, tossing dirty clothing around for a moment, and then came running back out.

"Richard, do you have my keys? They're not in my bedroom where I left them last night." *They've been in the same place for years,* he thought.

"No I don't have them. I haven't seen them! Quick, girls, help find Dad's keys."

Mary looked down at Misty and continued to sob. "She doesn't look good, Rich. She's heaving now and her breathing is really shallow."

As the family went to pieces in attempt to save their beloved pet, Jakob slept soundly in his little bed. He lay in his familiar fetal position with his football by his side and a shiny set of van keys around his middle finger.

13
That Was the Last Straw

May 10, 1985

As daybreak enlightened the township of Clover Springs, a family was still reeling from the disappointing loss of their faithful pet, Misty. Even six months later. Mary was the one who eventually found Donald's van keys in Jakob's possession.

Misty had died on the front landing, just eight minutes before the keys were discovered. It was agreed that she probably wouldn't have survived even if they had gotten her to the veterinarian. Misty had ingested about a cup and a half of anti-freeze and the Sterlings knew that it was little Jakob who 'unknowingly' poisoned the dog. But the boy felt no remorse and the whole family questioned his motives. The little boy's actions were finally established to be a horrible accident, and they moved on with their lives.

Donald sauntered into Jakob's bedroom at 8:15. The child was sprawled out on his single sized mattress. He lay on his stomach and tilted his head sideways, where his mouth released a sinister sound of snarling mixed with a nasal, murmur. The forty-eight year old father was swiftly reminded of a National Geographic special which featured two new born hyenas in Central Africa. He nudged his son, just firm enough to wake him up. The boy's eyes slowly opened; they were a gentle shade of green. He licked the saliva from the corner of his mouth.

"Yo, Jakob, it's time to get up son. It's gonna be a big day." Jakob didn't move. "It's actually pretty nice outside. I think we're gonna have to barbeque up that giant chicken that I showed you yesterday, remember?"

Jakob, reluctantly, turned his body over and revealed a disturbing truth. As he changed his position, Donald saw some blood on the ivory bedsheets. Just a little, but he knew that the child was wounded and reacted instinctively.

"Hey, Jakob, what happened to you?" He quickly sat down on the bed to examine his son. That was when he realized that Jakob's eyes had switched colour to a darker shade of green. Bewildered and intimidated, Donald asked again. "Jakob, what's happened to you? Why are you bleeding?" He reached down and met his son's hand as they both lifted the boy's pajama tops. Jakob was stone faced, even upon the discovery of three stinging scratches on his stomach that stretched across to his ribcage. *He's not even crying*, Donald thought. He looked quickly at his son's fingers and could see that his fingernails were clean. This must have happened in his sleep and with ungentle force. *But why? How?* The blood on his ribcage was still fresh. This hadn't happened too long ago. Donald reached over and touched the wound and Jakob retreated back in uncomfortable pain.

Jakob looked up and scowled at Donald. He rubbed his eyes and swung himself off his bed. "You're bleeding Donald. It's bleeding on you too you know. You'll bleed when it's seven Donald. At seven you'll bleed even more than you are now. Don't touch my hurt Donald. You're gonna hurt too."

Jakob made Donald freeze like a statue and he couldn't even look down to see if there was more blood than he saw originally. It was hard to say with the boy's vindictive tone and although he was certainly speaking about his father's fingers, he still felt like he was injured as well. *And what's this seven nonsense?* He juggled the meaning in his head, but was mostly concerned about how he was being addressed.

"Donald will bleed too. I…am…hungry! Let's go…!" Jakob grabbed his football from the end of the bed, where it had lived for the night, and stormed out the bedroom and down the long hallway, past Mary and Amanda's rooms and into the kitchen.

"Jakob, why are you calling me Donald?" He caught up to his son and got in front of him where he crouched to his level. "I'm Daddy okay, Jakob? He nodded his head, trying to get a quick agreement. "You don't call me Donald okay bud? I'm Daddy, okay?"

"I'm hungry, Daddy. Please, can I have breakfast? I want Corn Flakes."

"That's better. Let's go and have some Corn Flakes then." Donald was appeased by the prompt change in attitude, but Jakob managed to roll his four-and-a-half-year-old eyes at his old man and stuck out his tongue when his father wasn't looking.

Mary was in the kitchen when they walked in.

"Good morning, Dad." She kissed him on the cheek and bent down to do the same to Jakob. "Good morning, buddy. How are you today?" Then she also noticed his eyes. "Dad, his eyes are really greenish-yellow today, don't you think?"

"Yeah, I was noticing that too. And look at this?" He pulled his son's pyjama tops up and showed Mary her brother's mysterious injury.

"Holy Crap, what did he do? That looks painful. He needs a cloth and some water, Dad." She grabbed a clean dish towel from the kitchen drawer and ran some warm water over top of it, until it was damp.

"Well, I don't know," Donald defended himself. "He doesn't look like he's in any pain. I don't know how this happened. I can't understand it either, but he's fine. He's not even in any pain for God's sake."

"Jesus, Dad, that's not the point. He could get a bad infection. Poor little guy."

"Okay, don't over react. Holy shit, it's not like I'm the one who did this too him you know."

Mary tended to Jakob's wound and raised her eyes to her father. "How did this happen then? His finger nails don't have blood in them. He didn't do it to himself."

There was a long pause and Donald felt an obligation to show his daughter his hands. He lifted his arms and turned his hands toward his daughter, who had an invested interest in the cleanliness of her dad's nails.

His nails were dirty, but not with applicable evidence. Or at least, free of any dried or fresh blood. Mary thought he could have washed his hands…easily. The markings were, at least, two hours old, she assumed. But her brother would surely be blaring bloody murder, if it were him. Nearing five years old, there was little progress in the relationship between Jakob and Donald. Or Richard, for that matter. He didn't do it, she finally determined. The scratches just didn't match the size of her father's fingers, and it would never be proven.

Mary threw her arms around her father. "I'm sorry, Dad. I didn't think you did it, really. I'm just confused, that's all."

"I know, sweetheart. I get it. But if it wasn't me, and it wasn't you…." He lifted the top, once again, and measured the four inch markings with his eyes. "I'm going to guess it wasn't Richard, simply because he's back in the city tying up some loose ends, and I don't think that Dee-Dee would be capable of doing this."

As afternoon pushed its way into the early spring day, Donald made an announcement to his gathered family, less Richard – *and Barbara, of course.*

"So, I told you guys we were going to do something fun this weekend, right?"

Amanda nodded and her eyes glowed with excitement.

"Well, Mary already knows because she helped me pack some stuff, but we're all going to the park to have a nice barbeque tonight.

I bought a big chicken yesterday and I think a nice night out together will be exactly what the doctor ordered, don't you think?"

"What park, Dad?" Amanda asked curiously.

There was a pause and Donald knew his answer was going to cause some controversy. "Well, I was thinking of going to the big park, on the other side of town. You know…the old property."

Amanda gasped, "What? Why do you want to go there, Dad? Mary, you don't want to go there do you?"

"It doesn't really bother me. That stuff is in the past Dee-Dee. There's nothing left there except for a big ugly stump for memories."

Donald chimed in, "I've been there already…with Jakob. It felt good when I was there. It kind of felt like I was closer to your mom, to be honest."

The whole time, Jakob sat quietly and spun his football in his hands, taking a break every ten seconds or so, to pick at the bandage on his ribcage. He seemed content with whatever the decision was and even cracked a smile when no one was paying any attention.

By half past four, the Sterling family pulled up to the park entrance. It was a familiar route for Donald and a distant memory for the girls. Jakob had just woken from a nap and was making a fuss, blurting out short, perplexing words and making unsettling sounds.

"We're here," announced Mary. "I kind of wish that Rich was here to see this, hey Dad."

Donald put the van into park and pushed the bridge of his glasses further up his nose. He then glanced over to the centre of the park and saw that there was a clean and vacant picnic table near the manmade fountain. It was situated in what used to be the backyard of their prior property. The giant stump, from the haunted oak, sat only thirty-six feet away from that spot, and Donald started to question his decision to come to the location.

After pulling the propane Hibachi out of the van, and handing Mary a plastic bag, Amanda took Jakob by the hand, and they all made their way to the chosen spot. Jakob clung to his football, and after re-acquainting themselves with their familiar surroundings,

Mary asked her little brother if he wanted to play some catch with her.

"Me too," Amanda begged. "We can make a big triangle and throw it back and forth."

This became a bit trickier than expected with the amount of newly budding branches in the way, not to mention the already green, spruce needles. As the three Sterling kids set themselves up, Donald prepared the barbeque and unwrapped the large, prepared chicken. After shaking some additional pepper on the bird, he reached down and retrieved a long, metal skewer, and some food clamps for an inexpensive, but effective, rotisserie.

As the children started to throw the ball to each other, Donald's head started to pound. He couldn't stop thinking about wanting a drink. Needing a drink. But luckily there wasn't any alcohol packed. It was probably a virus that he had picked up while shooting a baby shower on Second Avenue, the week prior. Nothing to be alarmed about anyway. He just needed an Aspirin and something non-alcoholic to wash it down.

Mary tossed the football to her little brother and Jakob failed to catch it, as per usual. The ball flew through the air and struck Donald on the thigh, before coming to rest on the ground beside him. He immediately felt the need for his anxiety medication, and reached into his pocket to retrieve it, but the meds were forgotten on the kitchen counter, back home. He reached down and threw the ball back to Mary, who was furthest away.

"Hey guys? If Jakob can't catch the ball, maybe you guys should change positions so the bloody ball doesn't come over here okay?" He was clearly irritated already.

The three Sterlings changed their spots and Jakob moved to within ten feet of the enormous oak stump which caught his attention. Their repositioning gave Donald a valuable opportunity to concentrate on how exactly to utilize his battery-operated rotisserie, and he attempted to fit it onto the miniature grill. *I can tell this is going to be painful.* he thought.

"Come on, Jakob, are you playing or what?" Amanda awaited his attention while holding the esteemed football above her head.

Jakob turned to Amanda and then quickly back to the stump and just stared at it. His quick, double take, fooled Amanda and she hurled the ball at her brother, where it landed early rolling up to his heels and resting, like it had been there all along. Jakob looked down and twisted his body to pick up his ball. He focused on Amanda, and brought both of his arms back, beside his head, flinging the ball toward his sister.

Meanwhile, Donald had figured out how the clamps tightened and prepared to stab his raw chunk of meat. He used his finest known judgement, and centered the skewer before forcefully thrusting the metal spit, deep into the thick bird. He lifted the skewer to secure the chicken evenly on the rod, and it was then that the ball, thrown by Jakob, miraculously flew over Amanda's head and struck Donald high on his shoulder. This made him flex his right arm habitually, and as he did, the family's mighty source of protein wiggled off its sword, and landed on the insect-infested ground. It rolled a foot and a half before coming to a rest, and Donald was infuriated. He had reached his boiling point and couldn't control his anger any longer His rage escalated, and his reaction was not only sudden but arguably uncalled for.

Donald examined the chicken on the ground and cringed. All three of the Sterling siblings stopped what they were doing and froze, awaiting their father's next move. He glared at the skewer, still tight in his right hand, and then back to the chicken. And then, without any preparation at all, Donald glanced over to Jakob and pounced to his right, spinning the skewer in his hand, like he was Master Jedi, Obi-Wan Kenobi. The steel-pointed rod came down hard on the little boy's pigskin, piercing right through its thick hide and deflating it immediately. The ruthless and brutal force of Donald's actions brought forth a dramatic, and noticeable reaction from his girls, and little Jakob flinched before inviting a dark and ominous cloud into his brain.

The shifted man's brow furrowed, and he clenched his left fist. He pulled the rod from the ground and the pointed skewer had penetrated the ball, clear through, at least eight inches. Jakob stood with his mouth hanging open and a tear began to well in the corner of his eye. Donald's head was ready to explode, but spearing the football had relieved any further tensions. Now though, he was burdened with the inevitable and immediate regret that he was expecting.

"Hey, Jakob. I'm really sorry about that. It was a mistake and I shouldn't have done that." Jakob stared and grimaced in emotional pain. "We'll get you a new one champ, I promise you."

The child made direct eye contact with Donald, and if he could have shot laser beams, he would have. He let out a guttural sound from his innards and rotated toward the converted oak stump. Without hesitation, he walked over to it and climbed on top. He kept his back to his family and crossed his legs, and arms.

Mary and Amanda's minds were instantly transported to the days of their haunting. Their little brother sat upon the stump of the tree that they saw a man in, at one time. The tree that caused residual sightings of Jimmy Murphy. He just sat there, like he was at home. He was saddened over the loss of his prided football, but satisfied and comforted at the same time. The enormous stump held a residual energy that little Jakob could relate to. He began to hum quite loudly and his voice drowned out the cool breeze.

The two girls were frightened, almost speechless, and Donald recognized a correlation to the past. Considering their disturbing location, and the sudden, drastic drop in temperature, it really seemed all too familiar.

14
The Interview

August 17, 1985

ESTHER Zerabescki entered the classroom and advanced to her solid, red mahogany desk. She had taught kindergarten and grade one children at the Clover Springs elementary school for nearly thirty-four years. A kind and unique woman, now in her mid-sixties, she readied herself for her next interview. It was with Donald and Jakob Sterling.

"Where did I put that damn pencil?" She adjusted her reading glasses and slid her chair back to check the floor. "Oh sure, there it is…Murphy's Law, don't you know." She bent over slowly, from her seated position to retrieve the writing instrument. Her bones creaked and she let out a breathy sigh. "Oh, Esther, I think it's about time to pack it in, old girl." She giggled like a young teen, but her hair was as white as the driven snow and gave her age away.

There was a hefty knock on the door; the Sterling's had arrived. Jakob was wearing his finest pair of blue coloured, corduroy pants, and a nicotine coloured dress shirt with a collar that sat funny around his neck. His crooked teeth were freshly brushed and his hair was combed by Donald himself. *Other than the non-stop bitching and complaining, it really wasn't too much trouble,* Donald thought.

Mrs. Zerabescki sat up straight and gave welcome to her next appointment. "Yes, please come in friends. Come in, and please sit down here." She motioned to two wooden gymnasium chairs that were placed in front of her desk like podiums at a debate.

"Mrs. Zerabescki, my name is Donald. Donald Sterling, and this is my son, Jakob." Donald sat down after shaking the teacher's hand, and pulled Jakob by the arm, guiding him to his chair.

"Welcome, Jakob. Would you like to shake my hand too?" The woman stretched out her arm and offered the five year old her hand in friendship. Jakob stared at the teacher's gesture, but failed to reciprocate.

"Jakob, be a good boy and shake the nice ladies hand." Donald was sensing an uncomfortable and embarrassing situation evolving. The boy looked at his hands, but they never made the gesture.

"It's quite alright, Mr. Sterling. If Jakob doesn't want to shake my hand, he doesn't have to."

"I'm really sorry about that, ma'am, he only woke up about forty-five minutes ago."

Mrs. Zerabescki coughed, covering her mouth with her clenched fist. "No need to apologize. I see all varieties of interesting children in my classes, Mr. Sterling. All different varieties, indeed."

"What is it, Mrs. Zerabescki that you need to ask us? We have some plans with the family at 10:30 this morning. My son, Richard, has a meeting with a local employer, at 1:45, and well… it's a busy day."

The experienced educator, looked at Jakob, and then back to Donald. "How is Amanda, Mr. Sterling? She was such a bright, young student."

"She's doing great, thank you. She's in grade nine now already, can you believe it. It seemed like yesterday that she was being taught by you."

"Grade nine? My goodness, how time has flown by. She was such a good student; such a pleasure to teach."

Then she brought up a sensitive subject. "I'm so sorry to hear about your wife, Mr. Sterling. She was such a talented author. I met her more than once you know. I just couldn't believe it when I read that she had passed. She really had a beautiful soul didn't she?"

"Yes, she most certainly did." *She really, really did. I miss her, so fucking much. Just don't say another word about her, lady.*

Esther got up from her chair and walked around to the other side of her desk. She lifted Jakob, gently, by his arm and brought him with her to the toy chest on the other side of the classroom. He sat and investigated the options for entertainment. Mrs. Zerabescki returned to her well-worn chair and shared a long and awkward stare with Donald. He pushed his glasses closer to his forehead.

"Mr. Sterling? How much, exactly, does Jakob there know about the 'strange' occurrences that took place in your old home? Have you had any conversations about those times?"

Donald was caught off guard, and hadn't realized how fast these stories could travel from one mouth to another, changing ever so slightly, every single time it was communicated.

"Well, actually, ma'am, Jakob has never been told about those days. We don't talk about it very often. It wasn't a very positive time in my family's life. He doesn't need the same sort of grief that we went through."

"I understand, Mr. Sterling. Of course, I understand." She noticed his hands shaking a bit, and laid the rules out. "I wouldn't anticipate any issues with Jakob, would I Mr. Sterling? That, I would say, is my number one regulation. We want a delighted classroom. The children have to be happy while in my care. Do you think that Jakob will show us a smile before leaving here today?"

Donald looked over to his son and swallowed the frog in his throat. "Well, he's been a bit of a challenge over the last couple of years. I won't lie to you. It's been tough without his mother around.

I've relied on my daughter's to help out a lot. We're doing the best we can though."

"Of course you are, Mr. Sterling."

"Maybe he's a handful every once in a while but he's a good kid most of the time."

"I'm sure he is, Mr. Sterling. What about his friends?" Each syllable that exited Mrs. Zerabescki's mouth stung Donald deeper. "How many friends does the boy have?"

The Sterling father began to perspire. "Uh, he likes to stick close to home. He's great friends with his sisters, Mary and Amanda." He waved his hand at the woman. "He doesn't really care to meet anybody new."

Mrs. Zerabescki turned toward Jakob and saw that he continued playing; now with a wooden steam train engine sporting four, shiny, red wheels. She held her head steady at the little boy and addressed Donald.

"Mr. Sterling, he looks quite normal to me. But you should know this. About five years ago I had a student, in grade one, who wrote a story called *The Freak Show*. It was all about your old house. The old Murphy house. We knew about the awful things that happened there over the years, but I couldn't believe that one of my students, a child, Mr. Sterling, would have brought such personal and unguided information into the classroom. Their parents were the ones who put this information into his head, can you imagine that? So many lies and exaggerations."

Donald was lost for words, but before he could even think clearly, Mrs. Zerabescki mercifully changed the subject.

"I think he'll be just fine here. He'll meet some friends and I'll make sure he's happy while in my care."

"Oh, thank you, Mrs. Zerabescki. I really appreciate you giving him the opportunity. It's exactly what he needs."

"Every child needs an education, Mr. Sterling. Every child needs a chance to succeed."

Donald smiled and stood up to shake the teacher's hand once again. "Thank you again ma'am. I'll talk to him and he'll be happy, I just know he will." He called to Jakob, who, reluctantly, dropped the train on the floor and made his way, bowing his head to the floor in disappointment.

"Goodbye, Jakob. I will look forward to having you in my afternoon class this year." She handed Donald a folded pamphlet. "Two to four, Mondays, Tuesdays, Wednesdays, and Thursdays. We'll have so much fun, and learn so many interesting things."

Jakob's arm stretched upward, and he was forced to hold Donald's hand on the way out of the classroom. The new student looked up at the old lady standing by the door and let out some noticeable gas from his rear end.

"Jakob, say thank you to Mrs. Zerabescki...please? Then we have to get going."

"Thank you, Mrs. Zerabescki."

Donald's shoulder's dropped and some nervousness was mercifully released.

"That's a good boy," the woman smiled. She reached into the side pocket of her long apron, and removed a few stickers and a yellow sucker. "Here you go, Jakob. These will be fun. You can tell me where you put them, when I see you again. Oh, by the way, I really like the colour of your eyes. So unusual and distinctive."

Jakob took a step out the door and suddenly turned back to his teacher. "I promise not to eat your bones. No, Mrs. Zerabescki, not even your bones will taste very good at all."

After an uncomfortable shared chuckle, the Sterlings left and headed back to their home on the south side of Clover Springs. They pulled into the driveway and behind Richard's small car. The proud father turned and looked at Jakob in the back seat. *The family was whole once more. Well...mostly*, Donald thought.

"Hey, Dad," Mary opened up the front door for her father and brother. "Well, do we have a school boy?"

Jakob scowled at his older sister and his eyes turned to a brighter shade of yellow again. Donald felt the hatred as the ambiance throughout the entrance and living area was disrupted by negativity. Her smile, upon greeting them at the door, had dissipated and turned into a truly gut wrenching, and overwhelming sensation of guilt, and she felt a headache coming on.

"So, tell us about it, Dad. What did Mrs. Zerabescki say?" Mary was still interested.

"Well," Donald confessed, "He's actually going into afternoon kindergarten. He'll make some new friends there. It'll be good for him. Maybe he'll surprise everybody and be one of the smarter kids…who knows. I think the teacher liked him."

Mary bent down, to Jakob's level. "Wow J, that's cool. You're going to be in kindergarten. Are you excited about that?"

"No," Jakob lashed out. "I don't wanna. School is for dummies. You leave me alone now. No more school for me." He ran down the hall, toward his bedroom, and right into Richard, who had just come out of the bathroom. The two of them hesitated and sized one another up.

"Whoa, slow down, bud." He picked Jakob up and lifted him high above his head, before letting the growing boy back down. "Where are you off too in such a hurry?"

Jakob's eyes shimmered an astonishing tint of yellow which was a result of a sharp reflection beaming off the artificial hall light. He lifted his left arm and pointed his finger high and into his brother's chest.

"You just piss off Richard. You are really, really sick, Richard… You are sick! I will make you too sick to breathe when there's seven Richard. You are sick!"

– *trampling off to his bedroom…*

15
Psychiatrics

September 8, 1985

"Enough is enough." Donald stormed into the living room to grab the phone book from the side table. "I'm telling you, this is bullshit, Rich. I'm Sorry, Dee-Dee, but enough God damn talking about it. I'm getting this kid to a doctor. Every fucking day this kid has to make my life a living hell."

Donald reeked of macaroni and cheese. Jakob had, once again, vomited all over his father's pants and it was quickly drying into a pungent, sickening mass on and around his crotch region.

"Oh, shit, Richard, look after this will yah?" He handed his oldest son the phone book and looked over to Amanda, cleaning some slobber off of Jakob's face. The little boy grinned and followed Donald, with his eyes. "I have to change or I'm gonna puke myself. Find me some sort of a child doctor in the city. He's got to be good, you hear me?" He disappeared, around the hallway corner, and into his bedroom to clean up.

Jakob had completed his first week of kindergarten with little to no incidents to speak of. His teacher, Mrs. Zerabescki, had no qualms and Jakob was interacting quite normally with the other children. The family was rather impressed with his early progress in the education system.

Richard had his usual headache while staying at the house. His leave from work in the city ended up resulting in a lawful termination as he couldn't commit to a return date. And now everything that he learned through his university courses were in danger of being squandered.

Richard's family needed him far too much. And his mother's life insurance policy certainly ensured that the family would never have to endure any further financial difficulties. But they would live frugally, as there really was no ethical reason to flaunt the money of the sadly deceased. Or at least, that was the right thing to think.

Richard thumbed through the yellow pages and found an advertisement for a specialist in the city. He was a psychiatrist by the name of Williams. K. Williams it said in big, bold print. It didn't ever say what the K stood for, but it didn't matter. Richard grabbed a pencil and wrote down the phone number for his father, who was cursing from his master bedroom. The smell of Jakob's lunch had filled his nostrils and penetrated his nasal cavities.

"I'm going to help change J's clothes too." Amanda was in charge of her brother today, as Mary had gone for a hike, with friends. "Oh, that's so gross Jakob. Why don't you tell me or daddy that you feel sick?"

"Don't be long Dee-Dee, Dad's probably going to call this doc…"

"Did you find a number Rich?" Donald interrupted as he exited the bedroom, with new blue jeans and slicked back hair. "I'm telling you, I'm done. Every time I get close to this kid, my own son, for God's sake, he treats me like I'm the anti-Christ or something. It's about time to get this shit looked after before he makes a big mistake that we'll all regret."

"Yeah, Dad. Here's a number for a shrink in the city. His name is Doctor K. Williams." *But he still didn't know what the K stood for…* "He's got years of experience. Been practicing for over twenty-five years already. I'd give him a try first and if that doesn't work, I'll look for another one for you okay?" He passed his father the piece of paper and placed the phone book down on the dining room table.

"Okay, I'm calling them right now and I'll leave them a message. They can get back to me, I'm sure."

"Dad, he's open on Sundays too. Maybe we can get him in today if you want to make the drive."

"Even better." Donald dialed the number. "Where is the little barf monster anyway?"

"He's in his bedroom with Amanda getting changed." Richard reached up and massaged his temples with his middle fingertips. "Damn this headache. It just seems to get worse and worse. I'm getting an Aspirin." He headed to the washroom's medicine cabinet.

"Yes, hello? I would like to make an appointment for my son." Donald spoke to a receptionist. "Yes, his name is Jakob Sterling and he's just five years old. Yes…yes…well, the sooner the better. Oh, he just started school… What's that? Oh, uh, what's the matter with Jakob? That's kind of a long and strange story ma'am." Donald continued to respond to the standard questions from the, thorough administrator's inquiries. "This afternoon? Well, I'm in Clover Springs. Yes, yes, it's a two hour drive… It's your only opening until Thursday? Yes, I understand. 3:45? I'll be there, thank you. Yes, thank you ma'am. We will see you then. My name is Donald… Donald Sterling. Yes, I have insurance. What's that? Sure, sure, I'll make sure to bring the card, thank you, goodbye now."

Amanda came out of Jakob's bedroom and the boy held her hand, sporting a new pair of corduroy pants and a thin, grey tee-shirt. Amanda had combed his hair back, but he had already messed it up, as a habit. Donald hung up the telephone and turned quickly to Jakob. They both caught each other's eyes and the aura in the room darkened again.

"Come on boy, we're going for a ride. Let's get your jacket on now. It's not too cold out, but I don't need some quack judging me about my poor fatherly skills either."

"Where are you going, Dad?" Amanda asked. Where are you taking J?"

"I've had it up to here, Amanda. I need to take Jakob to a doctor in the city today. Richard? Richard? Are you able to come with me? Dee-Dee, you'll will be fine here alone. Just until Mary gets home anyway, heh?"

"Yeah Dad, I'll be fine. I have a little bit of homework that I need to finish up before school tomorrow."

Richard returned from the kitchen. "What's up, Dad? You're taking him today?" Donald nodded. "Yeah, I can come along with you. I have nothing else going on."

By 1:27 in the afternoon, all three of the Sterling boys had departed to the big city for Jakob's, long overdue, psychiatric appointment. Whether he liked it or not, the young boy needed a professional opinion, and Richard and Donald were the most interested in finding out why his motivated hatred was, obviously, geared toward the two of them.

Back home, Amanda ran a bath and went to the linen closet to grab herself a fresh towel. She walked to the front door and locked the heavy dead bolt, knowing that the back door was already secured. It was just a habit. Now she felt comfortable so she went back to the bathroom and tested the temperature of the water. It would be ideal, but then an overwhelming feeling of love and affection swept over the fourteen year old. She undressed and used a match to light two candles around the tub. She looked in the mirror above the vanity and smiled. Then Amanda turned off the bright light and climbed into the bathtub.

The drive to the city was painful. Of course, it was Jakob who was responsible for that. He just wouldn't stop making noise, and it was eating away at the men of the family. Donald found himself speeding down the highway, just to lessen the driving time. *A ticket would be worth the risk*, he thought. At least he had his older and more reasonable son to talk to.

"Jakob, listen to me, bud." Richard tried to reason with him while Donald kept his eyes peeled on the road. "The doctor's just going to ask you a few questions, alright?"

"No, Richard, you shut the hell up," Jakob scowled, and continued to add to his brother's throbbing pain. "No one needs to listen to you so you need to shut up."

Donald lashed out and the van swerved, slightly. "Jakob, watch your mouth boy. Where did you learn that kind of language anyway?" He looked into his rear view mirror.

Jakob met Donald's eyes in the tiny rear view mirror and answered his question, confidently. "I leaned it from you, Donald." Both Sterling adults shivered as a result of the boy's words. Jakob was so matter of fact about nearly everything lately, as if his brain had matured overnight. He was a pretty smart kid, but this would prove to be a bit unsettling, at any rate.

Back home, Amanda lay back in the porcelain bathtub, while steam rose from the hot water. Her eyes gently closed and she cherished the calm and relaxing atmosphere. Her peaceful sensation eventually gained a steady and grating humming in her ears, and the inside of her eyelids became suddenly alive with lightning bolts, shooting in all directions. She was finally forced to open her eyes, as her curiosity finally gave in.

When she did, Amanda saw a small light, in front of the closed bathroom door. It quickly grew to a stretched out, and hovering, full bodied apparition. Its energy fed itself from the pounding of Amanda's heartbeat, and the light intensified. Amanda sat up straight, and her mouth hung open. She felt no shame with her naked body and comfort overcame her fears.

The ghostly vision showed its true self. It was the very same woman that Amanda had seen before. Cradling a new born child in a grey blanket, the glowing woman managed an infectious, and luminous smile. Amanda squinted at the brilliant light, but this time made an early assumption. It was something that she had always presumed anyway.

"Mommy? Is that you? I've been waiting for your return. Please talk to me Mommy."

Meanwhile, out of town. "It's good to be back here, I suppose." Richard looked around as Donald drove through the city. "It's in the plaza centre, two blocks that way." He had a pretty good understanding of the directions to Doctor Williams' office, seeing that his old office building was only six blocks west.

Jakob had fallen asleep, only ten minutes earlier, and Donald said to let him be. The quiet and solitude would be a nice change compared to the last two hours. But Richard knew, all too well, that this would only anger the boy more, when he was awoken.

Donald pulled up in front of an old, run down, office building. It looked as if it had been built in the late nineteen fifty's and never seen a renovation. Donald picked Jakob up out of his booster seat, and the boy moaned, but stayed asleep. Richard's new digital watch read 3:36. They were right on time. *Hurray for small miracles*, Richard thought. They entered the front door and the building was musty. Then up to the woman behind the counter. Her name plate read Gwennie.

In Clover Springs, Amanda was in shock. She was speaking with her deceased mother and it was very real. "Mmm-Mommy?" Amanda was literally paralysed. She sat in the tub and stared at the woman in front of the door, but couldn't move very much. "Mom? It's you, isn't it? You've come to visit me…just like Dortie used to." She glowed and a few tears left her eyes and rolled down her flushed cheeks.

The spirit bowed her head slightly and spoke up, but her lips didn't move, and her voice was monotone. *"Hello Dee-Dee. You're still as beautiful as always. I have been trying to visit you for the past few years, but, as you know, it hasn't worked out too well, has it dear?"*

Amanda shook her head back and forth, realizing that she could suddenly move her entire body without effort, like she had been mercilessly released by the rigid force. She noticed the bundle in her mother's arms.

"Mom, is that a little baby that you're holding?"

The vision of Barbara nodded slightly and confirmed.

"What happened to that baby, Mom?" She sobbed. "Whose baby is that? Why do you have a baby?"

"Amanda dear, this is your brother. He followed mommy to the other side."

"Why did that baby follow you? Why did you have to go away to the other side in the first place?"

Back in the city. "Excuse me miss....uh Gwennie. My name is Donald Sterling. I have an appointment for my son here, Jakob." He held the boy, draped over his shoulder.

The attractive secretary was chewing a stick of gum discreetly. "Yes, Mr. Sterling. We've spoken on the phone. It's nice to meet you. Please fill out this form and I'll let the Doctor know that you're here." She stood up, showing her long and attractive, curvy legs, and Richard's eyes couldn't help but follow her out of the room. *What I wouldn't do to have a piece of that,* he thought. But she was probably out of his league anyway. *I guess looks aren't everything.*

"We should wake him up, Dad. Give him a minute to gain his bearings. What do you think?"

Donald gave Jakob a slight shake and held him up on his feet. The boy yawned and slits appeared as his eyes opened slightly. It already felt quite uncomfortable for Donald.

"Time to get up, bud. We're going to talk to a really nice doctor now, and I want you on your best behaviour."

Jakob looked unimpressed, but some toys in the corner of the room caught his attention and he casually walked over to them, sat down, and started to play.

Gwennie came back, into the room and gave an update to the Sterlings. "The Doctor will see you in about five minutes or so, please have a seat over there and I'll let you know when you can go in." She winked at Donald and both he and Richard looked at one another with bulging eyes.

In Clover Springs, the spirit of Barbara Sterling had some gruesome news. *"Your brother was murdered, Dee-Dee."*

"Murdered? What do you mean, Mom? Murdered by who?" Amanda trembled.

"He was taken from us by his twin brother. He wasn't strong enough to fight back. And either was I sweetheart. Either was I."

"I didn't know, Mom. I really didn't know. Dad didn't tell us. He didn't say anything about this." She was angry. "Why didn't Daddy tell me about the other baby?"

"He didn't tell anybody, my dear. He really didn't want to sadden you more than you already were."

"How did Jakob murder your baby, Mom? Is he really as bad as he seems to be?"

The energy of Barbara Sterling glowed brightly and her head shook, slowly, back and forth. *"Oh honey...he's even worse. So much worse than you should ever have to know."*

In the city, Doctor Williams entered his examining room and shut the door behind him, after the Sterling's were invited in. "Mr. Sterling, my name is Doctor Williams, please, let's all go over here and have a seat at the table." He motioned to a short, round table in the middle of the room that was surrounded by four, yellow plastic chairs.

All Donald could think of was...*what in the hell does the K. in the doctor's name stand for?* "Doctor, this is my firstborn, Richard, and this is Jakob...would you like me to call you by your first name?" He hoped to finally solve the mystery.

"No, that's quite alright Mr. Sterling. You can call me Doctor Williams. That'll be just fine. Now then, what can I help you with today?" He looked over to Jakob, knowing that this appointment was all about him.

"Well-" Donald started to explain, but he was interrupted.

"Doctor, Jakob here is very strange," Richard chimed in. "He's swearing at five years old. He makes weird noises and pukes on my Dad. He doesn't like me either. He growls and hisses at me. Why is he so mean? What did we do to deserve his resentment?"

After a short pause, the psychiatrist responded. "Well, with all due respect gentleman, I believe I can certainly understand why Jakob is causing you problems."

The youngest Sterling daughter continued to receive an education at home.

"I'm afraid that there's a great threat, once again, Amanda." The memorizing manifestation continued to communicate with the stunned Sterling teen and Amanda began to shiver. *"Your father is in grave danger. And so is Richard."*

"Uh... what do you mean, Mom? What kind of danger are you talking about?" Her breathing became heavy and she shook like a leaf.

"You can't tell them, Dee-Dee. You can't tell them that they're in danger. If you do, you put you and your sister in harm's way. Stop your little brother, Amanda. Stop him without telling them. Don't let him have his way, Dee-Dee! He's connected to the past. He's tied to the Murphy family honey. Stop him, please."

"How do I do that, Mom?" Tears welled up in Amanda's eyes and she let it pour. She heard the back door open, and knew that Mary was probably home. The captivating light dimmed and the spirit of Barbara Sterling started to blend in with the wooden door. As her energy throbbed, she offered one more piece of advice.

"I'm fine honey. I haven't gone far. Just wake me up and I'll come home, Dee-Dee. Just don't tell them, honey. Stop him. Stop him, before it's too late. Beware of his seventh birthday, Amanda. Seven was his agreement with Jimmy. He's going to be a big problem." And with that, she was gone. Amanda was cold as she sat in the tub and the water's temperature had changed dramatically.

In the city, Donald was offended by the doctor's last remark. "Uh, okay, and what exactly is that supposed to mean, doc?"

"As you can see, he's right here Mr. Sterling. Your son can hear everything you say. He's five years old, and this is when his mind is most subjective and curious. If you say negative things around the boy, he'll generally appear to be negative...do you understand me?" Both Donald and Richard submitted and nodded. They knew that they were in no position to even question him. It was a good time to just keep quiet and let the professional do his job. He had made a good point, and Richard was a tad embarrassed.

"Jakob, come on over here my boy." The doctor stood up and grabbed a large writing pad from a cupboard. He then hurried to his desk to find a black permanent marker, and brought it back, placing it on the table. "Sit over here son. I have a game for you to play." He handed Jakob the marker and turned the writing pad in his direction. "Now Jakob, I would like you to draw a picture of your daddy, okay?" He motioned his finger in Donald's direction.

Jakob looked up to the man and frowned. "I don't wanna draw Donald."

"Right here, Jakob." He pointed at the pad. "Can you draw a picture of your daddy? He's sitting right here so you can look at him while you draw, if that will help." His statement didn't go over very well. An irritable presence seeped throughout the room and all seemed affected by the boy's demeanor.

The stubborn little boy looked over to Donald and pointed at him, letting the doctor know exactly how he felt. "Donald," he said. "Not Daddy... Donald."

"Yes, Jakob. Donald is your daddy. Can you please draw a picture of him?"

After a brief moment, Jakob looked to Donald, once more, and then put the marker to the drawing pad. He drew a large circle, for a head, and a straight line from the center of that, down, representing a man's body. He was drawing a stick figure, and that seemed impressive enough. He continued by drawing an upside down V to create the figures legs and then something strange occurred. Jakob drew another straight line, to signify the arms of the simple figure, straight through the large circular head. Satisfied, he placed the marker down beside the pad. They all looked down at the drawing for a moment and tried to make sense of it. Even the doctor was pleasantly surprised. He picked up the drawing pad and examined the simple picture for a moment.

"That's good," Doctor Williams applauded the young lad. "Jakob, why did you draw your daddy's long arms going right through his head like that?"

Jakob looked down at the drawing and shrugged his tiny shoulders at the man.

"Why did he do that, doc? Why did he draw my arms going through my head? What does *that* mean?"

Doctor Williams laughed. "Well, gentlemen, I think he's just fine. I don't think he's going to be a big problem to be quite honest."

16
Love is Eternal

February 28, 1986

NEARLY *six years,* Donald thought. That's how long it had been since Barbara had passed away while giving birth to Jakob. Donald sat on the sofa and couldn't get his late wife out of his mind. He was taking his medication on time, and every day, since the physician from the city prescribed it, even before the Sterlings had moved to Clover Springs. But it was tough, and as his family sat around him in the living room, Donald made an unaccustomed statement. He slipped on his winter boots as he spoke.

"I'm going for a drive, and I wanna be all by myself, before anybody asks me if they can come."

"Dad, are you going by a store? My head really hurts. We ran out of Aspirin and maybe you can pick some up. One way or another, I've got to release this pressure."

"I hadn't planned on it, Rich. Drive yourself to the store. Mary might even take you if you ask nicely."

"Never mind," Richard was too weak to argue. He had deteriorated, rapidly, since the afternoon that he saw Doctor Williams, almost six months ago. Donald was gradually getting worse too. He felt defeated and lonely. No different than any other time, he supposed, but something was really picking at him, and he pushed his glasses closer to his forehead, before leaving the house into the cold, late winter morning.

Jakob's tests had all come back negative. There was nothing wrong with the boy, according to the opinions of Doctor Williams and his colleagues. He was acting up because the family was sad and negative. That was what the good doctor said. Anyway. The boy didn't improve over time. He just got worse. And everybody knew it, but no one knew what they were supposed to do about it. Jakob was hastily causing fear throughout the family and fear was something that the family needed no more of. Fear had a funny way of tearing a family apart, when it needed to be closer than ever. That was a lesson that had been already learned.

Amanda was afraid of her little brother, ever since her supernatural conversation with her ghostly mother. She was cautious of his actions, while keeping the chilling secret from every single one of them. Even though she was told that her father and older brother were in danger, Amanda wasn't prepared to put her and her sister in peril, as well. Something would have to come to her. She just needed some more time. For now, though, she was content sitting on the recliner, in the living room, and watching a morning talk show with her sister and two brothers. It seemed much too peaceful for the first time in a long time.

Donald's destination was pre-determined. He knew where he wanted to go, before he even turned the key in the ignition. Wearing a warm, plaid jacket and a thick pair of gardening gloves, he pulled up to the only place that brought him closer to Barbara. The old Murphy property. The emotional turmoil seemed to subside, if only for the time he was present in the park, but that was good enough for him. At least it was a start.

The large family park that had given a number of people colossal happiness, and scratched away at the evil that the location once possessed. He parked on the side of the road. There were no other vehicles around. Perhaps he would sit alone and reminisce. That would certainly make him feel better. It was his head, really, that needed some sort of a break.

He entered the park and his eyes immediately went to the far corner of the property. The large, imposing stump was only an illusion in Donald's mind. He saw completely different scenery when he looked. Each branch was still evident. Sticks, protruding in all directions and bare, from the cruel winter's lack of compassion. He saw riches and rubbish when he looked at the stump, and the stump, never once, even cared. He had already ruined any chance that he had with his young son at this very location. Crushing his cherished football and perhaps his dreams along with it.

Donald closed his eyes and lifted his head to the sky, inhaling deeply and taking in the cool, soothing air. He scanned the park with his eyes and could see only one other visitor. He was an older gentleman. Upon first glance, Donald could tell that he had seen this man before. Maybe at the grocery store, or perhaps in the short bank line up at one time. Regardless, Donald hadn't been much of a talker. He never made much of an effort, meeting new people, since he moved to Clover Springs. He might be responsible for his loneliness, but really, his life hadn't been without a fair amount of challenges over the years. There really was no excuse.

The elderly man sat alone on the park bench. He wore a tan overcoat and a pair of galoshes. His experienced face was carved with deep, cavernous wrinkles and his ears had grown, twice the size that they used to be at one time. He sat hunched over, wearing gloves with the fingers missing, and threw seed on the ground in front of the bench. After each donation of seed to the ground, he looked to his right and let out a bellyful chuckle. In between those moments, he only coughed and wheezed.

"Uh, excuse me, sir." Donald bothered the older visitor. "I couldn't help notice that you were tossing some seed down for the birds."

The man flung his head up to Donald and smiled. He was missing some teeth and this added to his oddness. "Well, hey there stranger. I'm feeding the ducks, don't ya know? These ducks are hungry, just like you are sometimes pal."

Donald glanced at the frozen grass and couldn't resist challenging the fellow. "Uh, mister, there aren't any ducks here. It's too cold for them right now. You're just throwing that seed away, I think."

"Well that's just some bullshit there." The old man was ready to prove Donald wrong. "I come here all the time. I'm always feeding the ducks here, don't ya know? Sure, there's no ducks here *now*. But they'll come back. They always do. Should be pretty soon, I figure. This here seed isn't goin' anywhere pal. The birds will get it eventually." His logic actually made a lot of sense.

"Why are you here, mister? Why are you feeding the ducks today?" Donald found that he had nothing better to do, but converse with the senior citizen. He was reminded that he had no friends in Clover Springs.

"Well, my wife made me come, to tell the truth." He motioned to his left. "Here, have a yurself a seat if you like. We're stayin' for a little while, I reckon."

Donald saw that the man was making no effort to move to the right of the bench, and he remained, contently in the middle. He thought about his option and stood his ground, as the outcome would have been quite awkward in his mind.

"No, I'm fine just standing, thanks. I've been sitting all day." *His pants were on fire, there was no doubt.*

"Suit yourself, pal" He looked up and into Donald's squinted eyes. "Hey...I know you. Or should I say, me and the wife knows ya. You're that Sterling fella, aren't ya?"

Donald was caught off guard. He had lived in Clover Springs for a number of years now, so it was a little bit embarrassing to admit to the old man that he was correct.

"Uh, yes, I'm Donald Sterling." He looked the man up and down. "Excuse me for my ignorance, but how do we know each other? Have we met before? I thought that you looked familiar. I don't get out much now a days so I don't see very many people."

"You used to live here! Right here on this here property, with your family. I remember it like it was yesterday, I tell ya. Your boy got sick here too, didn't he? The *'freak show'* was never as famous as when you Sterlings lived here. I tell ya."

"How do you know all that? Who, exactly, are you?" Donald was puzzled. For the first time since the incidents that took place at that same location, he felt violated. How did this old man know about his family's woes? It was never in the newspapers, or television, as far as he could remember, anyway.

"Me and the wife have been following the goings-on here since the 1940's pal. Me and the little woman know every little thing that happened here. Even the names of the ducks pal…all of em."

Donald wasn't cold anymore. The adrenalin that had built up from the timeworn man's words had warmed him with dread and an anger began flowing through his veins once more.

"Me and Gladys think yur pretty brave, Sterling. And yur pretty wife. Barbara. It's hard to believe she even put up with you during those times."

Donald nodded. He knew the responsibility and burden during those days rested on his shoulders.

"Well, she was pretty brave too, God rest her soul."

"How did you know that Barbara had passed away?"

"She was a pretty good writer too. I read one of her books, ya know. Yup, not too long ago either."

"Again, how did you know that my wife died?" Donald was stern with the man, testing his hearing.

The gentleman laughed slightly and threw some more seed on the ground. "My wife, Gladys told me. She tells me just about everything. That's where I get all my information pal. Gladys is my rock."

Donald paced, back and forth, creating a three and a half foot indentation in the grass. His footprints, carving their pattern into near frost.

"Okay, I'm listening. But hurry up and get what you have to say off of your chest. I could use a drink." The words left Donald's mouth for the first time in months. His brain had told him that a scotch may have to be a top priority after this conversation was over and he had made his way back home.

"I don't think yur crazy, pal. Gladys told me that your place was haunted." He looked around and chuckled. "The place that was right here. Right here on this spot too." The old man grinned largely and cradled his tongue like a cobra, ready to strike. "I can imagine what you've been through pal. I believe in ghosts ya know. Gladys made me believe. These things don't usually, totally go away, you know that right? Sometimes these things last for an entire lifetime too. I've seen it before Sterling."

Donald stopped pacing and stood directly in front of the man, whose face had an unusual pigment and appeared blue when cold. "You may know a lot, old man, but with all due respect, you don't have a God damn clue about what happened in that house."

The gentleman struggled to stand up, but he managed, and straightened his back to address Donald, face to face. He came within inches of Donald's stare, and they shared each other's carbon dioxide. He spoke slowly and gently, almost whispering to Donald, but he was also belittling him at the same time.

"Don't be so fuckin' naïve, pal. Your wife, Barbara, was a talented artist. She wrote a fuckin' memoir about your experiences in this here Murphy house, now didn't she? It was called *The Pale Murphys* now wasn't it? I told you that I read one of your wife's books, didn't I? Well didn't I?" His voice suddenly raised and it caused Donald to nod, quickly. "My wife, Gladys, read the book too. Your wife is a local celebrity pal. Don't be so fuckin' blind."

Donald had forgotten about his wife's final book. He had started to forget about almost everything, it had seemed. The old man was right. Donald became rigid and started to shiver, all of a sudden. The warmth he felt, only minutes ago, was gone. Guilt flooded Donald and he gained his wits.

"Well, I should get going. You're right mister. I've been so caught up in my own bullshit, that I haven't even taken the rest of the population into consideration. I've shut down and it's all my fault. Thanks for the blunt eye opener mister, I appreciate it, believe it or not."

Donald turned to walk away and guilt overcame him.

"Now just wait a minute there pal. I'm thinkin' you should know something before you go."

Donald stopped and turned back to the old fella. He was intrigued with what he was going to say next. "What is it? Do you want to make me feel worse or something?"

"Gladys says yur in danger." He sat back down in the middle of the bench. "She says that yur wife, Barbara, has a baby. The baby had a message that it shared with yur wife, and yur in danger, pal. You better fuckin' watch yur back cause' the message is all about the number seven."

Donald mustered up the courage to confront the cocky, wise man. "Well, it seems that your wife, Gladys, know it all, huh? She knows my past, she knows my future? Listen, can you do me a favour? Again, with all due respect, you just tell her to mind her own God damn business, okay?"

The rugged, elderly soul, chuckled again and looked to his right before peering back at Donald. "Well now, isn't this a sad and emberrisin' situation. She's been sitting right here the whole time buddy." He stretched his arm out and positioned it on the top of the right hand side of the bench. "Why don't ya ask her yurself? I'm sure she'd like to debate with ya, don't ya know."

After a long and truly uncomfortable pause, there were no more words to say. Donald walked down the worn path that used to be his driveway, and back to his awaiting red van, parked on the street. His entire short ride home he thought of the little old man's words. *He wasn't crazy.* His wife had passed on and she was sitting beside him on the park bench, during a late winter morning visit to the park. She was helping him feed the ducks. Who was Donald to judge anyway?

When he entered his house, it felt a bit different than it had before. It was quiet and cold. He first saw Amanda as she was drinking a glass of milk at the dining room table, so he looked for confirmation.

"Hey, Dee-Dee, where is everyone? Is it cold in here or is it just me?"

"Hi, Dad. Jakob is napping, Mary took Richard's car and went to a friend's house to watch a chick flick or something. And Richard is downstairs. He's not looking to good, Dad. I think he's getting sick. He wanted me to tell you that he wanted to see you when you got home. And yes, it's cold. It's very, very cold. Can you fix that please, cause' I'm gonna need more blankets to sleep if you don't."

Donald kissed his daughter on the forehead and headed down into the basement. There, he saw his son, Richard. He was sitting at a card table that was set up in the middle of the rumpus room. The table had a bottle of scotch and 2 rocks glasses, filled with ice cubes on it. Richard made eye contact with his father and picked up the bottle, which he poured the contents into each glass until they were both four fingers deep with the addicting solution.

"I've been waiting for you, Dad. I can't take the little bastard anymore. He puked on me today for no reason at all. Just because he hates me. That's why. He even stuck his finger down his throat, Dad. He meant to do it." He handed a glass of scotch to his father, who pulled out a chair and sat down with his son. "We need to fight this together, Dad. If we don't, he's going beat us and he'll be the winner. Help me stop him. Please…I'm losing it here…" He lifted his glass high in his father's honor. "Cheers!"

17
Teacher's Pet

October, 30, 1986

"YOU, my boy, are the perfect vampire!" Donald referred to Jakob's, cheesy Halloween costume. "Great job, Mary, he scares the shit, right out of me. Hey Rich, look at your brother." He snickered.

"Yeah, not so loud okay?" Richard had tied one on with friends the night before. His head was hammering on top of the already continuous pounding...*pounding, pounding, pounding...* He wore a black, long sleeve shirt, and a pair of royal blue, baggy sweatpants.

Mary put her arm around her younger brother and smiled. "Yup, he's scary, alright. It's amazing what some Brylcreem and plastic teeth can do for a guy. He was good too. It only took about a half an hour to get him all ready. And no messing up that make-up on your face either J. Cause then it wouldn't look real anymore."

Jakob stood, unamused with his family's antics. His hair was slicked back, just like the stereotypical look of Count Dracula. He wore a dark, black cape and was even coached to speak, like the infamous vampire himself, but Jakob wouldn't probably embarrass himself like that. He didn't really care if others liked him or not.

He seemed to only be motivated to make the lives of his father and brother a complete living hell.

"Did you help out too, Dee-Dee?" Donald asked Amanda, as she exited her bedroom, clearly still groggy.

"What are you talking about?" She looked down at Jakob, "Uh, no, I just got up." Amanda continued to steer clear of her little brother, ever since the soul of Barbara had told her that Jakob was dangerous, and she couldn't alert Donald and Richard because she would be doing more harm, than good. "Dad, don't forget, I'm going to Kelly's Halloween party tonight."

"Oh yeah, right, Are you going to be dressing up this year? You've worn some pretty great costumes."

"No, I don't think so. It was optional and I'm too old for that stuff now. And what am I going to wear anyway? All the costumes are totally lame, and it's not like anyone cares about that stuff anymore, Dad. Halloween is just for the younger kids."

"Here's your apple, J." Mary said. Jakob reached out his hand from inside his cape and took the piece of fruit from his sister. Every kid in Mrs. Zerabescki's grade one class was required to bring one juicy apple for the party at the school today.

"What's up with the apple?" Donald asked. "Since when does Jakob like eating fruit?"

"He needs it for the party Dad. It's for the tub. Their bobbing for apples, aren't you J?" Mary was still somewhat invested in her brother's wellbeing. He hadn't caused a panic in her yet. It seemed like a delicate part of his master plan.

"I am Dracula," he tried to speak clearly with his, glow in the dark, false, vampire teeth. "I vant to suck your blood." He walked quickly, around the corner, and went straight into his mother's vacant office, which was seldom accessed and almost never used.

Little Jakob had remembered his sister, Amanda, looking for a Band-Aid in the top drawer of her mother's armoire in this room. He saw something useful in there. Maybe now was a good time for him to take full advantage. He glided the drawer open, and exposed Barbara's sewing kit. It was full of different colour threads, and sharp, single eyed needles. He reached in and collected three, two-inch, needles and quickly closed the drawer. Donald still hadn't cleared away Barbara's things. It was too painful and her memories were kept, unappreciated, for none to see.

Jakob set his maroon backpack down on the ground and listened as his family continued to converse about some boring subjects that didn't pertain to him. He pulled the big, shiny apple out of his bag and proceeded to stab the sewing needles, deep inside, penetrating the bright red skin and continuing through to the white, enriched fruit itself.

One from the top to the mid-way point. One from the bottom, straight up to meet the other and a third, deadly needle, he pierced through the right hand side. Jakob ensured that the heads of the penetrating needles were flush and un-noticeable, and then placed the apple into a side flap in his backpack before leaving the room and shutting the door behind him. He walked to his family.

"Okay, Vlad, It's time to go. Are you done terrorizing the village and sucking the blood of the innocent peasants?" Mary was in charge of driving him to school. "Say goodbye to everyone."

Jakob put on his rubber boots and a thick, winter jacket before leaving through the back door. Mary smirked and followed him to the car, but Donald just kept telling himself that the boy only forgets to say goodbye. He's too excited and just doesn't remember. *Ignorant son of a bitch...*

Mary pulled the car up in front of the Clover Springs elementary school. She parked and got out, followed by Jakob. The school was crawling with ghouls and goblins, witches and clowns. (And the odd fairy and policeman.)

A determined Jakob had remarkably breezed right through his kindergarten year. No problems at all. The other children thought that Jakob was mysterious. They didn't care too much that he wasn't very social. In fact, Mrs. Zerabescki thought that Jakob was fitting in just fine with the others.

"Morning, Jakob, did you remember your apple for the basin tub?" The teacher bent down to ask at his level.

Jakob nodded, and a slight sneer crossed his lips.

"Oh, super! That's really great! You look so scary, Jakob. I quite like your costume. Why don't you go over and put your apple into the water like a good boy."

"Good-bye, Jakob. I'm leaving now. Have fun." But Mary was ignored so she smiled and acknowledged Mrs. Zerabescki before she left.

"Children… children, listen up now, please. I would like everyone to gather here in a circle." The twelve kids, all dressed in their Halloween garb, ran over to the teacher and created the desired circle. Something they had done a hundred times before, it seemed.

"Now then children. Everyone remembered an apple for the basin tub except for Oscar. Luckily, I happened to bring an extra one, so you can have one too. Does that sound good to you, Oscar?" The awkward boy shrugged his shoulders and nodded his head up and down. "Okay then children. First I want to go around the circle and share our costumes with each other. After that we're going to bob for apples, and that will be today's snack. Does that sound good to everyone?"

The children all cheered, and even Jakob was excited and couldn't wait for the festivities to begin.

After a humorous journey around the circle, Mrs. Zerabescki was educated by her students. On this day, her classroom consisted of a princess, two pirates, two wicked witches (including herself), a vampire, some sort of a strange robot, a mummy, Robin Hood, a policeman, a kitty cat, and a boy who dressed up as a nurse. Oh, and of course there was Oscar. He wore a pair of Groucho Marks eye-glasses with the fake mustache and thick eyebrows. That was about it for his costume. They were all excited for the following day where they could trick or treat and fill their tummies with candy.

"Alright now children, I want you all to make a straight line behind Jillian in front of the basin tub. The rules are easy. You step up on the stool and put your hands behind your back. You have to grab one of those apples using only your mouth, do you all understand?"

Everyone did, but there were a few of them who were ecstatically happy that they weren't first. It would be shy and meek, Jillian. Her chances were good, if not great.

Jakob stood about half way through the lineup. He never let on, not even once, that there was a dangerous apple in the basin. And he wasn't worried about his chances of getting the bad apple either. It was the most fun that the little boy had all week. He watched, as, one at a time, the children bobbed for their apple. It didn't matter if you got the one you brought. They were all the same anyway. Most were red, but there were three green and two yellow ones as well. Some of the students struggled and some found it to be quite easy, but Jakob watched, as each one of them, took the first bite of their fruit. Jakob's apple was a bright red, so it helped in narrowing down his anticipation level.

Now it was Jakob's turn and there were only six apples left in the tub. The one infested with sewing needles was one of them. Jakob knew that his white face make-up that Mary worked so hard on, would be washed away, but he dunked his head and pushed a yellow apple, up against the side of the tub, biting down hard and lifting it out to a 'golf clap' session of the usual applause. He took the apple out of his mouth and stared at it before holding it to his side.

"That's a good boy, Jakob. Great job! Okay, Oscar, it's your turn now. Step right up and take a turn. Let's see what you've got, Groucho."

The young lad took his glasses off and stepped onto the stool. He was hesitant at first, but submerged his head and came up with a shiny red apple. As the other children clapped, Mrs. Zerabescki walked up and grabbed the apple out of Oscar's mouth.

"Now you see boys and girls..." She spoke like the wicked witch of the west and made sure she had the class's attention. "Oscar here forgot to bring an apple today, so I think this is my apple, isn't it?" She loudly cackled and a few of the children cowered.

Jakob watched in expectation, as he realized that his teacher had the bad apple, but he wouldn't say a word.

"You can go again, Oscar. There will be an apple for you too, but this one's mine, thank you very much." The children all laughed at Oscar's expense and then they fixated on their teacher as she licked her lips.

The aging educator brought the apple up to her wide open mouth and bit down firm. One of the sewing needles grazed her upper lip and it was enough to cause her to wince in pain and cry out. She dropped the apple and spat the piece that she had bitten onto the ground; a few drops of blood followed. The children all started to panic, but the teacher was quick to run to her desk and grab a tissue, which she held tight to her mouth.

It was quiet for about thirty seconds. The students all stood, stunned and confused. Mrs. Zerabescki blotted her lips with the tissue and moved back to the bobbing station, picking up the discarded apple, on the way.

"I want to know, right now, who brought this apple to class?" The children all stood around silent. No one would take their eyes off of the flustered adult. "Now, damn it! Who brought this apple to school today? Children, somebody had better speak up, I'm telling you right now."

Oscar was the most relaxed, but the other children were frightened by their teacher's tone. She was serious and a few kids even cried. Little six year old, Jillian, peed herself. Jakob was the only one who showed no remorse. He stuck out like a sore thumb. The other children started to turn their heads toward the Sterling boy. Each student who committed to the move made it much easier for the next to follow.

"Jakob, did you bring this apple to class today?" She pulled out one of the three needles and held it up to his face. "You realize, young man that if you brought this apple into my classroom, there's going to be big trouble, mister. Now I'm only going to ask you one more time, Jakob...did you bring this apple into my classroom today?" She shoved it into his face.

Jakob looked up to his teacher and his eye's glowed an all too familiar shade of yellow.

"Yes I sure did, Mrs. Zerabescki. Cause' I vant to suck your blood."

Back at the Sterlings' residence, Donald was partaking in a drink. Even for him, it was early. Richard was still sleeping and Amanda had just left to her friend, Kelly's house, for her party. When the telephone rang, it was Mary who rushed to answer it.

"Hello? This is the Sterling's residence."

"May I speak to Mr. Donald Sterling please?"

"Sure, who may I say is calling?"

"This is Principal Douglas Saunders, and I'm phoning from the elementary school."

"Oh my God, is Jakob alright?"

"Please, let me speak to Mr. Sterling. Unless this is Mrs. Sterling. I guess I should have asked." The principal recognized that he had made an awkward mistake and tried to conceal his ignorance. "Oh wait, I'm terribly sorry. I just remembered that Mrs. Sterling passed away years ago... please forgive me."

Mary yelled for her father to come to the phone. It didn't sound good to her and it would surely sound worse to her father. He sauntered out from the bathroom, where he was combing his, salt and pepper hair, and he held a high-ball glass in his right hand. It was 11:14 am.

"I'm coming, tell them to hold their horses. Why does the bloody phone have to ring when I'm trying to relax? It's probably a tele-marketer or someone trying to sell some sort of shit."

Mary held the receiver out to her father. "It's Jakob's school. It's his principal, and he doesn't sound too happy about something."

Donald paused, and knew that the following news was not to tell him that his son had won the costume contest at the school today. He took a breath and cleared his throat.

"H...Hello, this is Donald Sterling."

"Mr. Sterling, this is Principal Douglas Saunders calling from your son's elementary school."

"Okay yes, what is it." Donald prepared himself for the worst possible news.

"I need you to come down and pick up Jakob right away. We need to talk about his expulsion from this facility."

"Expulsion? What are you talking about? What did he do that was so horrendous, Mr. Saunders? Jesus, who's ever been expelled in grade one?"

"Mr. Sterling, did you give Jakob an apple to bring to school today?" The principal was looking for more people to lay blame on.

"Uh, I think that my daughter, Mary, gave him an apple, yes... from the pantry. I saw it too. It was a big, red one, I believe...why?"

"Okay, Mr. Sterling." The man's voice started to crackle from a rush of adrenalin. "I think we have a real problem here. It may be in our best interests to get the authorities involved here."

"What in the hell are you talking about? I'm on my way. You'd better explain yourself a little better when I get there, you hear me?"

Before he hung up, the principal had one more thing to say. For some reason, he felt the courage to stand up to the angry father and offer him, yet another, dire warning.

"I remember the stories of you and your family, Mr. Sterling. At that...'*freak show*' that everybody talks about. I've got news for you, your son, Jakob here, is the '*freak show.*' When your son came into my office today, he sent some damn shivers down my spine. He has no empathy. He has no conscience. He doesn't care about anything, Mr. Sterling. Not even about himself."

18
An Explanation in Futility

January 8, 1987

The New Year -1987- would be the year of change. It was ten years to the day that the horrors at the last house began for the Sterling's. That was the day that the family moved into the old Murphy house. It seemed like so many nightmares ago, but the reality was obvious. The future had arrived and they were still being plagued by misfortune and despair. This year though, everything would surely change.

Jakob was expelled from school. It was concluded that the boy purposely meant to harm his teacher. Namely, Mrs. Esther Zerabescki. The school board dismissed any supplementary accountability for the other four members of the family, when Jakob himself admitted to the deed, and even explained, in great detail, how he cleverly positioned the needles into the apple. *He smiled and found pleasure in his account.* So it was years of home schooling for Jakob and it was all too familiar to Donald, who home schooled Richard with Barbara, after he had come home from the hospital in 1979. Educating Jakob was going to be a challenge though. He was quite intent on making his family miserable, and it was creating a mutiny amongst the other members.

Mary had a pretty good idea of what was going on. Her intuition could sense some spiritual energy in the house. Not like the old house, mind you, but *some* energy, to say the least. Without knowing Amanda's secret, Mary was well aware that her little brother was a bit disturbed. She often wished for a second opinion from the one they were given by Doctor Williams, but she never brought it up. There was something wrong with Jakob, and it worried her sick. Her most vital concern was that it couldn't be fixed.

The eldest Sterling daughter was twenty-two years old now. She didn't have a man in her life, *or a woman, for that matter,* and felt that her family were too dependent on her availability and were dragging her down. She felt she was wasting away the most precious years of her life. Mary remembered living in the city, when she was young. *Before all of the sorrow.*

When it came to Richard, he had a similar emotional state to Mary. He was a witty and confident gentleman, but Richard was in a different position than Mary. He knew that Amanda held a secret that she wasn't sharing and he was witnessing the peculiar behaviours of his little brother, first hand.

The pale-haired 'miracle child' was twenty-four and nearing his twenty-fifth birthday, in less than two months. He really never had anyone in his life, other than his immediate family. His brief education was being squandered, and his job in the city was a distant memory. Clover Springs was far too small to share his skill set, but it was so much more than that to Richard. He felt that he owed his father.

He owed him for getting through his own illness while he was sick and in a coma. Those were two painful years that the younger man was forced to withstand. But Richard would say that it was the most enlightening two years of his life. It appeared that he was educated in his sleep. He had a different angle on reality and it intrigued him, to say the least.

But Richard, too, was losing hope. His youngest sibling despised him. He hadn't felt that sort of hate since…well, since he was – *younger.* To make matters worse, he enjoyed the scotch now. It helped him with the headache that he was far too stubborn to go and see a doctor about.

Fifteen year old Amanda Sterling was the key. She held on tight to the hopeful resolution that the family craved, and also the shattering calamity that seemed inevitable. She was not as optimistically cautious any more. It was red alert, and she never took her eyes off Jakob anymore. Amanda knew that she was the last hope and it would be up to her to stop her little brother before she harmed someone in the family. *But how?* There were no easy answers, but it was on her mind while she lay in her bed, late on a brisk winter's Friday night.

Everyone slept, or that was Amanda's assumption. But she wasn't able to, no matter how much she tried. She wasn't sure what the problem was, but something was bothering her, more than usual. It might have been the fact that her older brother had, selfishly, mimicked the sickening behaviour of her father and carried around a glass of scotch, most of the day. There was a distinctive possibility that her little brother was the cause of all this. Poor little Amanda just couldn't understand why.

Or it might have been the secret that she was keeping from everyone… *That,* she thought, *was it.*

She decided to listen to some music. That usually put her to sleep at night. It had worked for years. Amanda opened up her bed side dresser drawer and pulled out her Sony Walkman. She could see, almost clearly, from the bright light that was emitting from the moon and shining through her window. She wasn't interested in listening to the radio at that moment, so she clicked open the cassette compartment and pulled the tape out. She squinted to ensure it was the choice she wanted and pushed the cassette back into the machine. It was her favorite band, Bon Jovi, and in went her ear buds. She immediately felt some relief of her thoughts and tried drifting away.

An Explanation in Futility

At half past one in the morning, Amanda was fast asleep. Her music, still played, gently in her ears and it was set to repeat, which it had done once already. The final track on the tape cassette finished for a second time, and before the music restarted again, a static and low frequency message started to play. At first, Amanda wasn't stirred, but after thirteen monotonous minutes of the repetitious beckoning, Amanda woke up and was immediately alarmed.

"Amanda? Amanda, my sweetheart, it's your mommy. Talk to me, honey." And it continued to repeat. *"Amanda? Amanda, my sweetheart, it's your mommy. Talk to me, honey."*

Amanda opened her eyes wide as the majestic sound of her mother's voice resonated through her earbuds. It was the most peaceful tone that she could imagine.

"Amanda, Amanda, my sweetheart, it's your mommy. Talk to me honey. Amanda, Amanda, my sweetheart, it's your mommy. Talk to me, honey."

The teen was nearly petrified. She ripped the ear buds away and threw them onto the bed as far as the thin wires would let her. There was no sound and no lights and no electricity. There was no horror, and only an acceptable sensation of exhilarating satisfaction. She then quickly retrieved the head phones and replaced them into her ears. The voice continued.

"It's your mommy. Talk to me, honey." The same message repeated, over and over again. Amanda found the courage to reach out to the disembodied voice. She knew that her mother might have some more information for her. Some information that would allow her to come to terms with Jakob. Maybe she would have a valuable strategy and some fundamental intelligence. The teenager interrupted the repetitive call and pulled her head under the blankets.

"Mom it's me, Dee-Dee. I can hear you, Mom." The girl spoke under her breath so she didn't wake her family, and the echoing message finally terminated immediately.

"Amanda dear, I must speak to you like this. We don't want the others to know. We can't afford for your father to know about these visits. No one can know, sweetheart."

"But why, Mom? Why can't they know? I can't keep this secret anymore. It's driving me totally crazy, Mom. Everybody is falling apart again. I don't know what to do and it's driving me mad."

"They mustn't know, Amanda. Even if they beg. It's a matter of life and death, honey. You don't have much time."

Amanda listened intently and had difficulty telling whether she was asleep or not. "Okay, Mom, I'm listening. Tell me what to do."

There was a short pause, and Amanda listened to the sound of the tape as it revolved around the spools, inside of the cassette player.

"Dee-Dee, things aren't like they seem. You and the rest of the family are confused, my dear. Your brother, Jakob, possesses an even greater danger than what you and the rest of us faced in the old house. Do you remember?"

Amanda bobbled her head in agreement, but no one was there to see it.

"I'm trapped here, honey. Like Dortie was, and her Mommy and Daddy."

"Who's trapping you there, Mom? Is it Jakob?"

"No...well, not exactly, honey. It's what little Jakob has become. He's not who you think he is, Dee-Dee. He's not Jakob, as you know him. He has a different personality than a young boy his age should. The personality lives inside of him. In his brain, honey. It lives in his mind and plagues his innocent soul."

Amanda closed her eyes and thought of the ordeal at the old Murphy house. "Mom, help me understand. Are you trying to tell me that Jakob is doing the same things to Dad and Richard that Jimmy Murphy was doing to them in the old house?" Her voice was cracking and some words were higher pitched than others.

Once again, the tape ran for five seconds with no sound. *"No, honey. What I'm telling you is that Jimmy Murphy is still doing this to your Dad and Richard. Jakob is just the carrier. He's the host and Jimmy Murphy still remains the parasite, feeding off your emotions and causing all of this turmoil."*

"I thought that Mrs. Prescott got rid of Jimmy Murphy, Mom. I thought he was gone for good. Why is Jimmy Murphy still in our lives?"

An Explanation in Futility

"So did I, Dee-Dee, so did I. But there's an even bigger problem sweetheart. A problem that none of you should have to face." The voice through the earbuds continued. "You won't be able to stop him, Dee-Dee. You don't have the strength."

"That's okay, Mom. Dad has the strength, and Richard right? They're both big and strong."

"No, my dear, they don't have the strength either. No one has the strength. Not even when you put all of your strengths together."

"What can we do about this, Mom?" Amanda started to cry, fearing that her family was finally doomed.

"This doesn't have to happen, Amanda. All you have to do is wake me and all will be back to normal. You're nearing the crucial timeframe, my dear. You must act before seven. Seven is the key, Amanda. Once he is seven, his soul has been sold to Jimmy Murphy."

"What do you mean, seven? You keep telling me about seven, but..." Amanda had an awakening and then abruptly understood what her mother meant. She changed the subject as she needed clarification on her mother's first point. "And *'wake you'* Mom? Where are you sleeping?"

"I'm right where you left me, sweetheart. I really haven't gone anywhere at all."

"I don't understand you Mom, please help me understand. I can't do this alone." Her weeping was becoming loud and she imagined that others could hear her now.

"Amanda, you have to protect your brother, Richard. He's in danger again, but you can't tell him. And your father. Your father, Dee-Dee. He is in grave peril. I sense that seven will be soon. You can't warn him though. Whatever you do, don't warn them. There's nobody to help you with this predicament. You must protect them all by yourself. You are strong, my dear. You always have been. Use all your strength and fortitude and stop him somehow. If you don't, he'll eventually get all of you, Dee-Dee. He'll eat away at all of you, one by one."

"But how am I supposed to do that, Mom?" Amanda sobbed and tears rolled down her face and onto her blue, flowery sheets. "I don't know what to do. I need you Mom, please help me. I don't know what to do. What's going to happen to us?" Amanda pulled out one of her earbuds and pulled the covers back while she listened for her family, but it was quiet.

"I can't help you anymore than I already have, sweetheart. Just remember, this is only real in your own mind. Everything you and our family is going through is the result of your own imagination. I'll be right here for you, Dee-Dee. Be there for your dad and brother before it's too late."

Amanda sniffled and took a deep breath. "Do you think it might already be too late, Mom…? Mommy…? Mom?"

And with that, the static on the cassette tape played for an additional twelve seconds before it clicked to a stop and the spools stopped moving. Amanda opened her eyes and looked over to her bedside alarm clock. If her mother was really just in her head and was telling the truth, then she had more to think about before falling asleep again. Maybe when Amanda woke up, it would all be over… but then again…maybe not…

19
What Comes Around Goes Around

May 14, 1987

MORE than four months had passed with little incident. Amanda would remain on high alert, and heeded her mother's words from beyond the grave. She kept quiet to her family, but needed to keep everyone on a short leash. It's not like Richard and Donald would notice anyway. They were loaded most of the time. Sometimes they were together and sometimes they were apart. Richard swore that it helped his headaches, but then he would wake up in the morning (or early afternoon) to complain about another *fucking* headache. He was only fooling himself in the end.

The youngest Sterling daughter sat in the living area. It was quarter to ten in the morning, and Jakob walked into the room. The faint hairs on Amanda's arms reacted to an instant blast of energy and reached out in all directions. The boy stood about three feet away from his sister and sulked before addressing her.

"Where is Donald?" Jakob asked with confidence.

Amanda shifted all of her attention to her little brother and swallowed before answering. "He was getting into the shower, I think. He just got up... why do you ask, J?"

Jakob started to snicker and turned to leave the living room. "I promise I won't eat his bones, Amanda."

He hiked round the corner and down the long hallway, out of his sister's sight. Amanda was quite concerned with Jakob's abnormal question, and the even more disturbing remark afterwards, so she got up to follow him, but was cut off by Richard, who was coming in the front door after shopping for some new toiletries. He was up earlier than usual today and he grabbed her, spinning her around.

"Oh shit, Dee-Dee, I have a splitting headache. Can you get me a cup of coffee?" He stood right in her pathway and obstructed her mission.

"Move, Rich, I need to see what Jakob's doing." She made a move to the left and Richard grabbed her arm. "It's okay, Dee-Dee. Jakob's a big boy now. You don't have to watch him twenty-four/seven anymore."

Meanwhile, Jakob had walked to the end of the hallway and opened the unlocked bathroom door, releasing a mass of hot and clammy steam from Donald's shower. He entered, ensuring that he hadn't been followed, and then quietly closed the door behind him.

Amanda continued to struggle with her eldest brother. "Rich, let me go. I have to check on Jakob."

"Whoa, okay." He let her go, but she hesitated before she proceeded. "What's your problem today, Amanda? Maybe you need to go back to bed or something if you're going to be bitchy."

"I told you, I need to see what Jakob's doing." She broke free of Richard's intrusion and briskly ran around the corner, into the lengthy, lonely hallway. But Jakob was nowhere in sight, so Amanda quickly started opening the bedroom doors. First, the door to the left. It was her room. The door was cracked open and the light was off. It was empty and she hastily moved on. Panic began to overtake the teens conscience.

Second room on the left was Mary's room. The door was closed and Mary had already left for an early morning job interview at the old, Clover Springs Co-op. Amanda opened the door and looked in, but it was empty too. The linen closet to the right was completely ignored. Jakob could have fit in there, quite easily, but after looking into Jakob's abandoned room, Amanda had a funny sensation. *I know where he is*, she thought.

It was the door at the end of the hall. Amanda knew that her father was showering, and could hear the water cascading from the shower head and down Donald's body. Jakob asked where he was. *How stupid*, she thought. Those precious wasted seconds could have been all the child needed to cause their father great harm.

By now, Richard had followed his sister and watched her as she opened up the bathroom door. More of the moist steam escaped and Amanda squinted both of her eyes to better her visibility. Jakob came running from out from the fog, screeching like an injured animal, and straight into his bedroom. He sat down in the corner with his knees up, around his chin and kept his buttery eyes peeled for an enemy.

"Jesus." Donald whipped back the shower curtain and stood in shock, buck naked. "What in the hell is going on out here?"

Almost in sequence, Donald and Amanda both looked at the fogged up mirror above the vanity. It had been drawn on by the tiny fingers of Jakob Sterling. In the short time he was in the bathroom, he drew his stick figure again. A large circle for a head. A long line for a body, and an upside down V for a pair of legs. But there it was again. To the absolute horror of both Donald and Richard, who had already seen that frightening and uncanny depiction of his father, one too many times. The long line for the arms, was sketched, right through the stick figures head.

"What is that, Dad?" Amanda had never seen the infamous drawing.

Donald grabbed the nearest towel and shut the water off. Richard's heart palpitated and he felt ill.

"Holy shit, Dad. That's the same drawing that he did at the doctor's office. Those arms are going right through the man's head again. What in the holy hell does that mean, anyway?"

Richard, had had enough. He huffed and spun to his right, taking three steps down the hallway and stood in front of his little brother's bedroom. Jakob cowered in the corner and a tear dripped from his right eye.

"What the hell is the matter with you? You have to stop doing this shit. Why do you hate us so much? What did we ever do to you Jakob? All we tried to do was love you, right from the start." Donald and Amanda froze, at the bathroom's entrance. "Say something, God dammit!"

"Rich, stop!" Donald reprimanded his son and wanted him to put an end to his verbal abuse.

But Richard continued, "Don't just sit there, Jakob. I've had enough. You aren't going to cause this family anymore grief, do you hear me?"

"Richard," Amanda yelled out at him. "Stop! Dad said stop! You're scaring me. Please stop."

"Maybe it's time for someone to give you a real good spanking. Don't just sit there and look at me, Jakob. Come here, I'll give you something to cry about you little son of a bitch. Don't give me that cocky assed look either. I'm not putting up with it today."

Richard appeared insane; he had finally snapped it had seemed. His rage was overwhelming, and he lashed out at his six year old brother, once and for all. He ran toward the corner of the room and was primed to pick the boy up and give him the lickin' he deserved.

Jakob held his arms out in front of him like a football player, blocking a tackle. Richard was thrown off balance and tossed back onto the small, single sized bed, which scraped along the hard wood floor and slammed into the wall. Richard's head made contact with a side table and the oldest Sterling sibling cried out in pain.

Donald, wearing his towel, and Amanda, rushed to the bedroom to see what had happened. Richard lay, crooked on the bed, and his extremities had all tensed up, causing his body to cramp. He couldn't even move and everybody looked at Jakob while he stared down at his tiny hands.

"Jakob? What are you doing?" He struggled to turn his head. "Dad, I can't move. What's happening to me?"

Jakob lowered his arms and placed them at his sides. Even he was amazed at his new found abilities, so he stood up and smirked at Richard, who remained nearly paralyzed. His eyes turned a golden shade of yellow and they glistened from natural moisture.

Donald's anxiety through his veins, and Amanda shook, horrified and helpless. The father of four felt that he needed to think quickly.

"Jakob," Donald yelled at his son. "You need to stop that right now. What are you doing boy? You're hurting your brother."

To Donald's astonishment, the simple, but aggressive command worked. Jakob ran out of the bedroom, and avoided Amanda as she reached out to stop him, but her attention immediately went back to her eldest brother.

"Rich, holy cow, are you alright? What just happened to you, are you okay?"

Richard could move again. He was freed once Jakob left the bedroom. He took some deep breaths and sat up on his brother's bed. The dire situation was coming to a head and Richard was all in.

"I'm okay. He trapped me somehow. He's tried to do that before. I've felt that heaviness before. I've felt that captivation. He's mastered his craft, Dad. He's officially dangerous and we have to stop him. He needs to be stopped. We need to lock him up, or something."

"Yes," Amanda sounded off. Yes, Dad, Richard's right. We have to stop him. He's dangerous. He wants to get you, Dad. He wants to get you and Richard. He's going to get you guys. You have to do something."

Donald looked over to Amanda and cricked his neck. "Dee-Dee, what in the hell are you talking about?" He pushed his glasses closer to his forehead and looked at his daughter as if she'd spoken out of turn.

Amanda knew that she had spoken out of turn. She wasn't supposed to say anything. "Uh... never mind. What are we going to do, Dad?"

Jakob had run from his bedroom to a strategic hiding place under the dining room table. He acted like he was an uncaged animal and the entire family was, beyond startled; afraid of the consequences.

"Jakob, come here right now." Donald tried to reason with the young lad, but he was having no part of it. "Don't be scared Jakob, I'm not going to hurt you son. Maybe we can go and have some ice cream or something."

The boy lashed out and pounced from under the table, growling and screaming at Donald like a trapped wildcat. He ran past more of his family's outstretched arms and into the bathroom once again, slamming the door shut and locking it behind him. Richard was the first to try the door, but it was, most definitely, secured.

"Jakob! Open this door! You're in big, big trouble mister. What are you going to do? Huh? Do you think that maybe you should come out here and apologise? Everyone deserves an apology, Jakob."

Jakob screamed from the washroom. "Richard, fuck balls! You are sick, Richard!"

"What did you say, you little shit? Maybe you can wash your mouth out with soap, while you're in there."

"You are so sick, Richard." The boy yelled some more. "You are sick and you will die Richard. You die fuck balls. You are so sick. Richard is sick. Richard is so, so sick."

Donald and Amanda joined Richard at the locked door and listened to his verbal diarrhea.

"Jakob, please open the door." Amanda tried to get through to her brother. "If you come out, I'll give you some candy. If you don't want ice cream, we could have some candy. What do you say, J?"

All went quiet in the bathroom. The family all took turns putting their ears up to the door, but silence ruled. After a few minutes had passed and the Sterlings talked among themselves to devise a solution, the distinct smell of smoke resonated from the crack at the bottom of the bathroom door. Amanda was the first one to notice and puckered her nose to inhale deeper.

"Dad, I smell smoke. It's coming from the bathroom and look… it's coming into the hall."

Richard grabbed the copper door knob and shook it feverishly, but it was to no avail. "Jakob? Open the door buddy. This isn't funny anymore."

Minutes seemed like long hours and everyone started to rattle in their skin as the fire got bigger and the smell of acrid smoke charged forward, polluting the hallway.

Donald had run out of options, quickly. "Get out of the way. I'm breaking the God damn door down. Jakob, stand back. Stand away from the door. I'm breaking this door down right now."

Donald rushed the door with his shoulder, but stopped before he made contact. He bounced on the balls of his feet for a moment, and then forcefully used his left foot and kicked the door wide open. A curtain of smoke rushed out of the bathroom and once it cleared, the family could see that Jakob was no longer in there. He had just disappeared into thin air, it had seemed. Panic officially had set in.

The bathtub was empty and the window was open with his bath stool underneath of it. On the floor was a towel in full blaze. It had already started to burn the tan coloured, linoleum flooring. Jakob had a preconceived plan. He had wadded up some toilet paper and placed it on his, very own, Incredible Hulk towel. He found the matches in the drawer. Somehow he knew that they were there. But they were for the candles, when the girls wanted to have bathes. Jakob started the blaze, which grew quickly, then placed the stool, opened up the window and climbed out. The fall from there was at least four and a half feet. There was a definite possibility that the boy could have been seriously injured.

Chaos ensued and Richard stomped on the towel, trying to suffocate the blaze, but it was bigger than he thought and the flames started to lick at his pant legs. Following up, Donald unwrapped the damp towel from his waist and body slammed the fire. After a few tense moments, the Sterlings were all satisfied that the blaze was finally out.

Their immediate attention reverted to Jakob and his whereabouts. Donald ran to the window and looked down. He wasn't there. The three of them positioned their troubled heads together to devise a plan, but before they could, Mary stood at the other end of the hallway. She was holding Jakob's little hand. He stood at her side, crying and shaking from apparent shock.

"Why does it smell like smoke in here?" Mary didn't wait for an answer. "Dad, why are you naked with everybody looking at you?" She shielded her eyes while Donald fitted himself with yet another piece of terrycloth.

"Jakob just told me that you guys locked him up in the bathroom. He said that you're sick, Richard. He kept repeating it, over and over again. I don't know what he's talking about, but I'd have to agree with him, from what I can see here."

20
A Drawing Says A Thousand Words

July 16, 1987

"We can't keep talking about this and not doing anything about it Dad." Amanda was furious and had no patience left as she argued with her father. She crossed her arms in front of her, and tilted her head.

"Yeah, I get it, Dee-Dee, but we can't just throw him in the trash bins behind the old mine, now can we? We can't put him on someone's doorstep and ring the doorbell you know. It's not going to be that easy."

"I'm not saying that, Dad. I'm saying that we take him to another doctor. Get him put into some kind of a home, or something." Amanda had just turned sixteen, and spoke with a matured confidence. "Let someone else look after him and maybe he'll get the help that he needs. You have to understand what I'm saying Dad. We're running out of time here. You know that Mom would agree if she was standing here right now."

"Okay, listen, I don't have the energy to argue with you today honey. I feel like a drink right now, so bad."

"You see, Dad, that's the problem. Maybe you don't have the energy to argue with me because you're drinking so much." She kissed her father on the cheek and headed into the kitchen to pour herself a hefty bowl of cereal.

Mary had a new job. She checked groceries down at the old Co-op on Third Street, and felt an abundant amount of independence, having some extra money to spend on herself for once. After a quick shower and a piece of toast, she was out of the house, borrowing her brother's car, and off to work.

Mary was scrambled by the claims that her family had made about Jakob. She didn't see it like everyone else did, and after the fiasco in the bathroom, two months ago, she was suspicious that her loved one's were all going a tad bit, *'whacked'* in the head.

Someone should have been a touch more enthusiastic about their birthday, arriving in less than twenty-four hours, but Jakob had no interest in cake and balloons. He was purely motivated by causing pain and hardship to the target of his choice. His priority had become malice, and his family was faced with the imminent, grim decision that couldn't be reversed. Richard, Amanda, and Donald were tremendously frightened. Their position on Jakob would constantly teeter between murder and suicide.

The blistering sun scorched the Sterling's house and made mowing the lawn uncomfortable for Donald. Even after Richard had told him that he would do it, once it got a little more bearable outside, Donald insisted on taking on the responsibility. It kept his mind off of drinking.

The problem was that Richard was hoping for the same thing. His skull felt like it was crushing his brain, and he truly believed that he was indeed sick, just like his little brother had informed him. He wanted a stiff drink too, and there was a fresh, unopened bottle of single malt scotch, down in the basement that was calling his name.

Jakob and Amanda were in the backyard together. It wasn't Amanda's first choice, considering the weather, but Jakob wanted to go out and play and Amanda wasn't about to leave him alone. She had made a deal with her older brother and her father. Each would take turns staying up in shifts to watch Jakob, while he slept. Amanda would read her mother's books and the Sterling men would drink and artificially quell their continual headaches. Donald had finally admitted that his head hurt too. *It was for as long as he could remember*, but his determination prevented him from complaining which would only further irritate his loved ones. Amanda gave up on Jakob after only eight minutes and demanded that the two of them find some immediate shade.

"Jakob, are you ready to go back inside yet? It's way too hot out here. I'm melting; aren't you?"

"Amanda, I really needed to ask you an important question." Jakob's grammar continued to improve.

Cautiously, the Sterling teen shaded her eyes from the rays of the baking sun with the back of her hand. "What is it, Jakob?"

"I think Richard is sick."

"Yes, I know, Jakob. You tell us every day…all the time. And that's not a question, Jakob. You didn't ask me any sort of a question."

"Donald is sick too. Donald needs to have a headache like Richard does."

Amanda lowered her arm and squinted. "What are you talking about? Don't say stupid things like that. Are you even serious when you talk like that?"

"You and Mary aren't sick, Amanda. You and Mary don't have a headache, right?"

Amanda grabbed his arm and dragged him inside. "Jakob, tomorrow's your birthday right?"

Jakob thought for a moment and then counted the fingers on both of his hands. "Tomorrow is seven, Amanda." He continued to scowl.

"Yes. Tomorrow *is* your birthday. You want that cool robot truck thing that was on TV the other day, do you remember that?"

The boy changed the direction of his mouth and smiled suddenly. Some brief excitement encroached on the little boy's face, and the dirty and dark mop on top of his head bounced up and down in delight.

"Well, you have to be a good boy, all day today and all day tomorrow, on your birthday too. Then maybe you're going to get that truck, Jakob. But if you're not good, you won't get it, okay?"

Jakob walked up the three stairs to the kitchen and saw Donald, sitting by himself, in the dining room. He stopped and looked back to his sister.

"I can be good today, Amanda, but tomorrow is my birthday and I will be seven. Tomorrow is the day that Donald gets to have his headache and Richard will be too sick." The meaning of seven suddenly became clear.

"Jakob, what do you mean 'too sick'? I'm not going to let you do anything to Dad or Richard."

After a long pause, the confused and clearly troubled little boy, sent chills down Amanda's spine. "Tomorrow Richard will be too sick to breathe."

By eleven in the morning, Richard was in the basement, watching television and refreshing his glass of liquor for the second time. The oldest Sterling sibling was a seasoned vet now. He could put them back like the best of them. Even better than his protégé, Donald. *Jesus, he only stopped drinking for eight hours this time.*

As soon as Richard touched the rocks glass to his lips, Amanda shadowed Jakob, as he descended the staircase leading to the basement. The boy walked unswervingly to his brother, and pointed his bent finger at him, sending him a truly and repetitive, disturbing ultimatum.

"Richard, you are sick. And tomorrow, you will be too sick to breathe!" An evil cackle came out of his mouth and he ran around the basement, playing with a few random toys that were laying around. He seemed so content and innocent, but he was successfully fooling all of them..

Amanda and Richard looked at each other and frowned. Richard took another sip out from his glass before toasting it toward Amanda. Courage flowed through his veins.

"Dee-Dee, if you wanna take a break, you go ahead. I'll watch the little bugger today. He won't be any trouble."

"Rich, what about the plan? What about us finally doing something about this? Don't you think, that maybe, we might be running out of time?" She looked over to Jakob who wasn't paying attention to any of the conversation in the rumpus room. "He's going way over the edge Rich, Seriously! You and Dad are in big trouble. The worst kind of trouble. The very worst kind," she whispered the last part.

Donald joined the rest of the family in the basement. He came prepared with a short glass, filled with cubes of ice. Amanda took a few deep breathes and started to tear up again.

"I don't understand why you guys have to drink all the time. It's disgusting. Don't you see that there's important things that need to be fixed here? It's only like 11:30 in the flipping morning," Amanda shouted. Even Jakob stopped what he was doing and glared at his sister. "I need to tell you something," she continued. "As soon as Mary comes home, I'm going to tell you all something that you need to know."

Jakob's ears perked up and he took a few steps toward his family. Richard held his glass in mid-air. It was heading to his lips, but his sister's boisterous command stopped him. Donald, on the other hand, had just arrived. He hadn't even partaken yet, but still reached out for the forty ounce bottle on the wooden coffee table.

"Listen, Dee-Dee, it's just a few drinks. To take the edge off, you know? It helps Richard's head..."

"No it doesn't, Dad. It doesn't help Rich's headache. It actually makes it worse." Amanda was furious. She felt that there was no other option than to take action against Jakob right now, but the rest of the Sterlings were entirely too pre-occupied to take any serious notice. *It was all the drinking...It was all the drinking. That's it*, Amanda thought. "That's it. Richard is sick. Donald needs a headache. This all makes sense now." *He's making them drink...*

Jakob bared his teeth and screamed at the top of his lungs. He ran toward Amanda and held out his hands, bending his fingers forward to mimic claws, and collided with his sister at full force, bashing her to the ground and knocking the air out of her lungs.

"You're not sick yet, Amanda. You and Mary aren't sick." He rushed up the stairs and Amanda started to cry once she regained her breath.

"Are you okay, Dee-Dee?" Richard stood up quickly and reached out to her, worried for her welfare.

"Uh…I think so. Please help me guys. He's going to kill someone. I can feel it. There's no more time. It's a crazy snowball that can't be stopped."

"Dee-Dee," Richard continued. "You have to tell us your secret. You need to tell us before Mary gets home. What is it, Amanda? What's this special little secret? Maybe we can help if you let us in on it."

"I can't tell you. He'll come for me. He'll come for Mary too. He'll destroy all of us if I tell you my secret. Please, don't make me tell you yet. Please, Rich."

Upstairs, Jakob went to the back door and unlocked it. He swung the door open, using an unusual amount of strength for a boy of his age, and proceeded outside. He looked in the corner, where the shed met the house and his delated football was visible under some leaves and a dirty tarp. It had been there since the appalling act in the big family park, more than two years ago. Jakob had brought it home with him, but it had lost its lustre, and it was soon disregarded. He reached down and picked up the gloomy and memorable mystery gift. It was cold in his hands, even with the blazing sun continuing to radiate down on the Sterlings' conflicted property.

He turned his attention to the black, propane barbeque up against the beige vinyl siding of the house. Dropping the football onto the ground, he noticed a thick, three foot piece of rope lying by the shed and picked it up, tying it around his waist. He then reached up, pushing up on the handle and swinging the barbeques lid over, where it slammed against its rusty hinges before it was able to make contact with the house. The smells of past meals permeated from the racks on the grill, but Jakob was only interested in one accessory. He used his lengthy reach to remove the filthy rotisserie skewer from his father's barbeque and he would quickly unscrew the sharp, food clamps. He held the rod down low and the clamps slid off and on to the ground. Satisfied, he carried his new weapon into the back entrance where he stopped and went into a stealth mode, ensuring he wasn't being watched. After wiping the dirty rod on his blue jeans, he swung the rotisserie skewer in the air, almost like he had practised sword training of some kind, and walked, confidently, down the hallway and into his bedroom. *He'll pay for putting a sword in my football...!*

Jakob could hear his family members still arguing down in the basement. He casually closed his bedroom door and admired the, still gristle covered, steel rod like it was a prized Academy Award. He then slid the sharp utensil under his bed and untied the rope from his waist before doing the same with it. Jakob crawled up onto his single bed, where he maneuvered into the fetal position and attempted to fall asleep for an unusual and early afternoon nap.

After five minutes, Amanda had ran up the basement stairs and into Jakob's bedroom. She pushed forcefully on the door and flicked on the light to see her little brother sleeping. She looked at her watch and it showed one in the afternoon already. He didn't even have lunch. No one has. Jakob slept soundly; like he had been there for hours. His snores sounded like the growling of a wounded fox.

Amanda contemplated her next move. No one was around. Now was her chance to become a hero like the spirit of her mother had pleaded. She glanced to the extra pillow on Jakob's bed and thoughts of extreme malice raced through her mind. She moved to the side of her brother's resting place and picked up the underutilized cushion, gripping it tight. Raising the pillow above her head, Amanda feared the repercussions of her actions and gave up.

I can't do it...I can't do it...I just can't do it. Her mind played her real intensions over and over again. "I can't do it," she broke down and wept, pitching the soft, but extremely deadly, pillow onto the ground beside her. Her little brother smirked while he slept. His own murder would never cross his developing mind, but for Amanda, the guilt would certainly never go away for as long as she was walking on this earth.

21
Hello Darkness My Old Friend

July 16, 1987

As the sweltering day progressed, the mounting tensions rose. Donald and Richard had passed out downstairs from drunkenness. It was seven in the evening now, and even Jakob was still sleeping. They thought that he must have been awfully tired, having napped for six hours already, but they knew where he was and he wasn't causing any trouble. Amanda and Mary, who was now home from work, made a simple, but effective supper, consisting of hotdogs and bread, with ketchup, hot mustard, pickles, cheese and enough mayonnaise to clog an artery. She wasn't to forget the mayonnaise. Mary was an expert at cooking the dogs in the microwave. She knew how to cut them, just right, so they didn't explode. They would even accompany the dogs with a handful of salt and pepper potato chips.

The girls continued talking in the kitchen. Amanda was filling Mary in on the current goings on with their little brother. Mary was concerned with her father and brother's drinking problem for sure, but it was all of the accusations that were being made against Jakob that clearly distressed her the most.

Amanda told her that Jakob had bowled her over and kept saying his alarming warnings, over and over again. Mary wasn't naïve. She knew that there was trouble, but hadn't witnessed the ominous behaviour as it had been described to her in great detail.

"I'm so hungry," Jakob said softly. He had come out of his bedroom, undetected, and made his way into the kitchen. "I want some food please." He spoke gently and Amanda sensed a hoax, right away.

"Okay, Jakob, here's a hot dog for you. Is one enough for now, or do you want two?" Mary was sympathetic to her little brother's hunger concerns.

"Two hot dogs, Mary. I need two hot dogs, cause' tomorrow I'm seven and I'm big and strong."

"Yes, you most certainly are." Mary said. Amanda slid a finished dog over to her sister who placed it on a plate with the other one. "Here you go buddy, enjoy."

Jakob nodded at his oldest sister and glared over to Amanda, as if to warn her and confirm that spilling her little secret will cause damnation on all of them. After licking his lips, he took his late supper and returned to his room without saying another word.

"You see, Dee-Dee, he's not as bad as you think. Maybe you are too immature, listening to the opinions of drunks and fools."

"I'm telling you, Mary, there's a real problem here." She grabbed her sister's hand as the microwave sounded and the smell of mystery meat filled the kitchen. "Come downstairs with me, Mary. We need to wake Dad and Richard up. I have something that I need to tell you all."

Mary was compliant, as she was more than ready to hear this magical secret that had been kept by her sister for many months. The hot dogs could wait because this was much more important. The girls scampered down the stairs, and into the basement where their brother and father were passed out, cold on the couch. They were a filthy mess amongst themselves and the house flies were gaining intelligence.

"Dad, wake up." Amanda nudged both of them. "Rich, get up, I need to tell you guys something...before it's too late."

Donald stirred and groggily, made eye contact with his daughters. "What...what's going on girls? Let me guess... something's wrong?" Richard also came to and sat up straight. He was already sporting a hangover at 7:30 in the evening.

"Okay, I don't think I need anything more to drink," Richard confessed. "Is Jakob okay or what?" He waited uncomfortably, for someone to speak. "Why are you all looking at me?"

Amanda was blown away by her brother's ignorance, as she stepped toward him and smacked him on the shoulder. "No guys, he's not okay." She shifted her direction and started her lecture. "There's a big problem. You both know it, but you're too flipping drunk to do anything about it."

The Sterling men stared at Amanda, as she ranted, and Richard reached down and poured an ounce and a half of liquor into his glass. The bowl of ice cubes had melted, but it make no difference.

"You see, Rich. You see what I'm saying here? Jesus, you guys make me sick. You just finished saying that you didn't want any more to drink." But Richard couldn't stop himself and even Donald was beginning to lick his dry lips.

"Dee-Dee, what's the matter with you? Since when do you talk to Rich like that?" Mary interjected. "I don't think that Mom taught you to act like that, did she?"

"You don't even see it, Mary. You guys are all blind." Amanda took a short break, and Mary sat on the reclining chair and waited quietly. *Waiting...waiting...wondering.*

"I wasn't supposed to say anything to anyone. I have a visitor sometimes. Like I used to at the old house with Dortie, remember?" Mary nodded and was intrigued the most it seemed. "Jakob has seen it too. But it's even more special than you think. It's the most wonderful thing ever, as a matter of fact."

Amanda started to cry and Mary reached over and grabbed her hand with her own. Donald watched Richard, out of the corner of his eye and couldn't resist, any longer, reaching across the coffee table and grabbing the bottle of tempting liquor.

She composed herself and carried on. "It's Mom. The spirit of Mom has come to visit me…like, at least four times already. She comes like a light, just like Dortie used to. She was so beautiful guys. Like a real life angel. We talk with each other and she tells me things that are really disturbing. Then she warns me that I can't tell you all. If I do there will be an even bigger danger."

Mary's mouth hung open while Donald and Richard wobbled, back and forth, trying to retain the information that Amanda was sharing.

"She gave me a warning. She told me a secret and I wasn't supposed to say anything, but now I'm afraid for what's gonna happen next."

"For God's sake, Dee-Dee, what is it?" Mary had lost patience. "We're here to protect you Dee-Dee. Nothing bad is going to happen to you. Let us know so we can help."

"She told me that Jakob was evil. She told me that Jakob was out to get Dad and Richard. That she couldn't stop it, but I had too. I don't know how…and she said that if I told you this secret that Mary and I would be targeted too. I think he wants to kill us." She was too loud. *"I think he's trying to kill us,"* she softly whispered. Richard made a strange, raucous sound and it came from his inner bowels, and the temperature in the basement dropped a few noticeable degrees. The entire atmosphere changed and stealth mode engaged.

Mary stood up and glanced up the staircase to ensure that Jakob wasn't eavesdropping. "You're telling me that you've seen Mom? As a spirit, Dee-Dee? And she told you that Jakob was evil?"

"I know this is a shock guys, but I had to tell you. You had to know, once and for all. I really can't bare all of this responsibility by myself anymore. It hurts my head and makes me nauseous in my stomach."

He was awake and active. The family could hear his footsteps, upstairs, but everyone froze where they were and contemplated 'Plan A'. Realizing, however, that 'Plan A' hadn't been formulated yet, the delay was much longer than anticipated.

Donald slammed back the last of his latest swill. It was his sixth drink of the day already, and he knew, somehow, that his addiction was being supported. Richard too was in denial. He couldn't believe his little sisters claims about his mother. He was completely immobilized during most of the dire experiences in the old house. Then there were the girls, who were ill-prepared for the immediate future: Mary with the new found, and implausible, information about her mother dancing in her head; and Amanda, like a sheep who stood in the middle of a circle of even dumber sheep. The wolf upstairs had stirred, skillfully and powerfully, setting his gruesome trap.

But there didn't seem to be any further warning for the family. Little Jakob made his way down the staircase and into the rumpus room, where his family was gathered.

Donald was the first to speak. "Hi, champ. What's up? You've been sleeping a lot today, huh?"

There was little interaction between anyone. Jakob wore a dirty pair of jeans and a wrinkled, black T-shirt. He was barefoot and his face was covered with ketchup and hot mustard. As soon as the hushed silence had become, far too uncomfortable, Jakob finally broke the ice and spoke up.

"Amanda, you wasn't supposed to tell your secret, don't you remember?"

Amanda stood like a sculpture, petrified by her brother's intelligence. Jakob took turns walking from one family member to another, and he started with an awestruck Mary.

"Mary, you are not sick, but Amanda told her secret, so now you're probably gonna get sick." He moved to his brother. "Richard, you are sick. And you have a headache all the time. Now you will be too sick to breathe." Richard placed his empty glass down beside Donald's and terror coursed throughout his entire body. *He wasn't the only one.*

"Jakob, what's the matter with you?" Amanda tried to get him to stop his nonsense.

Jakob turned his attention to his youngest sister. "Amanda, you are not sick. But you told your secret even though Mommy told you not to, so now you will be sick, I think. You're gonna puke all over the place Amanda."

Amanda shivered in dread and couldn't even speak or try to get through to her brother. He was making it difficult to think clearly, and they could start to feel it in the air. It was thick and it smelled funny. Like dust, cooking on a stove. Richard started to sweat and reached over, pouring himself another drink.

"Do you see how sick Richard is?" Jakob made his point, but Richard continued his pour. "And you Donald." Jakob made his way to his father and the commanding child scolded him like he was a hoodlum. "You are sick, Donald. You are not smart, like Mary. You are stupid like Richard. You are not my daddy! My daddy is dead, and you need to be dead now too, Donald. You and sick little Richard need to be dead too! It's okay though, because I'm here to help you all. I can make all of your scary feelings come true."

Both Donald, and Richard were insulted, but were too afraid to challenge their young family member.

"You are sick," Jakob was unrelenting. "And you broke my football, Donald. Now you need to sleep so you can be too sick to breathe."

Donald sneered, uncomfortably at his son and his mind wandered to a different place. A place, not that long ago. A time when he was with Barbara and they were making sweet love. The memories flooded his mind. Hundreds, *maybe thousands* of frames of information, darted through his contaminated brain, and he remembered something important. He looked at Jakob, intently, and the little boy waited patiently for him to process the new information, that grinded at his soul.

He had slept with his wife, only twice, during the last couple of years that they were together, before she passed away...*I really can't believe that she fucking died...* Both times he made love to his wife, he was sick. He was incarcerated by the evil spirit of Jimmy Murphy. He and Barbara conceived Jakob during one of those two times. It was the only math that made sense. But he was sick. He was really sick, and he may have passed his sickening genes through to his young son. *So that would mean...that would mean...*Donald couldn't even think clearly anymore. It may have been the liquor, or it may have been the drama, but he was so tired and his brain was telling him to let it go.

Jakob scanned the room with his greenish eyes and then he began to make a low snarl, deep from within his nasal cavity that resonated from his guts. It was already quarter to nine, and although Jakob couldn't tell time too well yet, he knew that it was too soon to act. It was not to be until his seventh birthday. That was his own internal command and no one knew that he carried his own secret. The contract was not valid until he was seven. *Not even yet...* With a huff, the little boy stomped away and up the stairs, retreating to his bedroom and slamming the door.

Two and a half drinks later, and after mixing his anxiety medication with his potent spirits, Donald was quickly retiring. They had spent the next hour telling each other stories and abnormalities about Jakob. It was official now as the entire family had given up on the boy. He had no friends, he was expelled from school, and his mind was full of hatred and anger. Jakob's mission was simple. It was pre-conceived. It was inevitable and the family seemed defeated, once and for all.

"Hey you guys, I'm really, really drained." Donald meekly admitted his intoxicative state. "Can we talk about this in the morning? We all should try and have a party for the little bugger, don't you think? I'm just kiddin'. We can't have a party, cause' me and Rich are too sick and soon we'll be too sick to breathe. What a crock of shit!"

It was Mary who rebutted first. "Dad, there may not be a tomorrow. Are you not seeing what's going on around here?"

It made sense to everyone, including Richard, who was three sheets to the wind, himself. But Donald was mentally exhausted. He couldn't fight anymore and he stood up from the couch and stumbled into the spare bedroom where his son, Richard usually slept.

"Wait, Dad." Mary ran after him and kindly assisted him into the bedroom. He sat down and Mary bent down to remove his sneakers. He had worn them all day, and the stench from his socked feet confirmed it. She removed his socks, as well, and quickly tossed them aside, turning up her nose. Guiding her father's head, gently to a pillow, Mary wept and sniffled.

"I love you, Mary. Tell your little brother that I love him. Tell him that I'm sorry that I wasn't a better daddy. You tell him okay, honey? And I love you too, Mary. Oops, I already said that. I mean that I love Dee-Dee and Rich too. And I wanna love Jakob too, but he makes it so God damn hard, doesn't he? Did I tell you that I love you too, honey? And I loved your mother too. She was the very best and you guys are lucky that you have her. Nighty, night, honey."

Mary nodded her head and bent over to kiss her father on the cheek. "I love you daddy." Amanda then came to the entrance of the room with a fear-provoking and fretful look across her face.

"HE'S COMING!"

The two Sterling girls watched their father as he slept, and within seconds they were interrupted by a sound: an all too familiar clatter of little feet making big footsteps on the stairs down to the basement.

This time his presence felt a little bit different. This time he appeared to have an invisible force of many helping him. An imaginary army to the rest of the family, but a strong, blood thirsty, full frontal assault to Jakob. And this time, as he growled and his sinister eyes turned an even brighter colour of yellow than they had ever been before, he stood confidently with a thick rope tied around his waist and a brightly shined barbeque spit that he clutched tightly, like a mighty dagger.

22
The Seven Year Itch

July 16, 1987

THERE was no point in trying to run away. And although their combined efforts could have easily overpower him, he possessed a great power that encompassed them all. The predictable was upon them and there was nothing that they could do. Amanda was horrified. She stood, right in the middle of the spacious rumpus room, and shook like a leaf. Her mind told her that she had failed to stop him. That metal rod in his hand was gripped with malevolence and his own conscience, would be the only thing to stop him now.

Mary needed no more convincing. She was sold, and she would have just about given anything at that moment to go back in time. A time before the move to Clover Springs. I time that she barely remembered...*but she knew that she remembered enough.*

Richard had come full circle. From a disgruntled and unappreciative teenage boy, to a truly dependant, and crumpled young man in a comatose state. *Two years to be exact.* And then a sick alcoholic who has finally met an enemy that he can't defend himself against. His own flesh and blood.

And Donald slept. The liquor had been too much. Eight drinks, even for a tall and healthy man, was enough to consider a long rest before the next day's tribulations.

Jakob huffed and puffed, like a mythical dragon, and all expected fire to spew from his nostrils. He looked in all directions and ensured that his simple escape route was easily accessible. After calming a bit, he stood between the rumpus room and the bedroom where Donald slept. It was now nearing ten in the evening.

"Donald is sick." The little boy was a broken record. "Donald needs a headache. He needs a headache so he can't breathe anymore."

Mary made a slight move in Jakob's direction, and her extremities ached. "Jakob, please give me the rod… please." She held out her hand, but he only cocked his arm, and pointed the sharp weapon directly at his sister.

"You don't get me, Mary. You stay away, cause' you're sick now too. Everyone can stay away now so I can help Donald get a headache." Jakob started to make his move toward the bedroom where his father was passed out.

Richard, through his drunkenness, tried to stand up straight from his seated position, but he rocked backward, ensuring he was sitting again. He looked down and put his hands on his thighs. They were heavy and his blue jeans felt like they were soaking wet, but to his amazement and wretched disappointment, they were not and suddenly, his eyes glazed over.

Amanda saw this as her opportunity. A chance to stop her brother from creating an atrocious mistake, and make her mother proud. That was her first and foremost priority. She ran at Jakob with her arms un-stretched and made a wailing war cry to distract him. The boy spun around and raised his hands, just like he had done in his bedroom two months prior. This time he held the long barbeque skewer in his tightly clenched fist.

She could see the veins protruding from her young brother's temples and neck, and before she was able to prepare herself, a mighty force, comparable to the strength of a mid-sized vehicle collision, propelled her backward and into a corner where she slammed up against a tall, contemporary lamp.

Again, Richard tried to stand up, and this time his adrenalin assisted him to do so. But Jakob had different ideas for him, and his next words drowned out the wails from Amanda and the efforts of Richard Sterling.

"You need to sit down, Richard." Jakob simply looked over to his brother and he was sent back, over the coffee table and onto the soft cushions again. His foot caught the bottle of booze and smashed it against the base of the couch, leaving the peppery and oaky aromas of scotch whiskey wafting throughout the basement.

"Jakob." Richard managed to speak from the side of his mouth. "You have to stop. You have to let us all go. Don't do th-"

"You are sick! And you will be the next one. You know why Richard? You know why? Cause' you already have a headache, so now you'll be too sick to breathe."

After a brief pause to wipe his nose on his shirt sleeve, Jakob turned back toward the bedroom where Donald had slept through all of the devastation in the rumpus room. There seemed to be only one hope, and Mary was in no condition to reason with such lunacy.

Mary was quite aware that she had to make an effort. "Jakob, please don't go." He stopped, turned and looked at her. "Come back to me and tell me a story. I heard that you saw Mommy too. Just like Dee-Dee. I want to hear more about that from you. Come and tell me about Mommy, Jakob." He turned back. "I was just thinking, Jakob. Maybe we could get you a new football."

Again he stopped, but only for a second, and then he proceeded to finish his business. Mary needed to pounce, and her internal audacity became their last ditch effort.

"Jakob, stop. You need to stop what you're doing right now!" She ran at him, but was stopped in her tracks by an unseen authority. She could move her face, her neck slightly, and her mouth still operated, but the rest of her was stone and inaccessible to her brain. Her inabilities made her clench her teeth together.

"I can't move! Oh shit, I can't move," she bellowed. "Daddy, wake up! Daddy, please wake up!" Tears flowed from Mary's eyes and no matter how loud she shrieked, Donald failed to respond. He couldn't respond. Jakob had made sure of that. *And what a good bartender he was.*

The boy made his final move to the door frame of the bedroom and as he stepped inside, the house began to shake and the lights flickered, *off and on.* Jakob, once again, was forced to stop his progress and turn to an astonishing sight. The clock read three minutes to eleven.

A colossal ball of light illuminated the base of the stairs. It was like going back in time for the Sterling family, and to a place that was all too comforting to them at one time, but also full of horror and exhaustive agony that carved their very identities. Quickly, the light dimmed and a full bodied light apparition appeared, making itself enounced.

It was a young woman in her mid-thirties, the majority assumed. She was very pretty, and hovered off the ground, about two feet or so. Her translucent body and chiselled jaw bone was embedded with an appearance of confidence and determination. Everyone in the room, including Jakob, trained their attention onto the shimmering specter and the resilient energy spoke down to the little boy.

"Jakob, don't you know what the time it is? Don't you know what day it is, my boy?"

Mary's eyes grew enormous and she managed an adoring smile. "Mom? Mom, is that you? It's you isn't it?" A whole new set of emotions overcame Mary and her heart started beating twice as fast.

"No, Mary," Amanda corrected her before her heart could be broken again. "That's not Mom. I don't know who that is. But for some strange reason, I don't feel scared anymore. What about you, Rich, how do you feel? Mary, what about you?"

Before they could respond, the ghostly woman continued her statement to Jakob. *"You haven't reached seven years yet, Jakob. That was your deal, wasn't it? That was what the contract read, wasn't it, Jakob? Seven years and not a minute sooner."*

The woman was right. It was still too early. But what a fantastic opportunity. There wouldn't be a better time, in Jakob's mind. But he couldn't yet. He agreed, and in return, he was granted a free pass, to stay away from the evil place. To live in harmony, with the uncontaminated and truly blessed, honourable spirits.

The glowing and mysterious woman had so much more to say to the imprisoned family. *"Jakob, you haven't held up your end of the bargain. It would be in your best interest to come with me now, before things get carried away, don't you think, my dear?"*

Then it clicked. In simultaneous epiphanies, the Sterling kids realized who the powerful and charming entity was.

Richard had sobered up as a result of the recent chaos taking place all around him. "It's you, isn't it, Mrs. Prescott? I can tell because you have the very same voice. You have a completely different body, mind you, but you have the very same voice."

Maria Prescott had returned. Just like she said she would. She was there to help, and it wasn't the first time that this family needed her assistance. She was even younger than remembered; and thinner too. Not as thin as she was at the end, before her untimely death, but thinner than when she had helped out before. Younger and thinner and happy and free. Her death had given her the autonomy she craved and ultimately deserved.

"Jakob, honey, you don't need to trap all of these fine people. Be a good boy and set them free. They just want to be free, Jakob, just like you. You have to understand that you're not out to get these girls. They've done nothing wrong, Jakob. Neither one of them. They've loved you and looked after you. I would say that you owe them now, don't you think so?"

Jakob held his steel rod tightly and scanned everybody in the room, sizing up his victims. He walked over to his youngest sister, still lying, awkwardly in the corner and pushed the metal rod close to her face. His eyes glistened and a evil smirk crossed his face.

"Amanda, she says I should let you go. You're sick now though. I can't let you go, I don't think."

"Let her go, Jakob. Show the entire family that you're able to compromise. Show them that you can make a trade. You let the little girl go and, in turn, time will go faster and it will be your birthday. Then, you will be allowed to see Donald and give him a headache."

Richard and the girls looked sideways at the spirt. She was manipulating Jakob into completing his dire act, in good time. It was just reverse psychology and the spectre's negotiating skills were very impressive, to say the least.

The insane little boy was puzzled. His precise control diminished when Mrs. Prescott's energy arrived, and his young age was easily influenced.

"Okay, Amanda. You can go and I will wait until my birthday. You go and get me something that I can use for Richard's headache...please?"

Amanda shifted her eyes and looked at the long, steel barbeque accessory. She knew that he wanted her to fetch yet another weapon meant to be used on her brother, Richard. All she could think of was calling the police and seeking municipal support.

"You go now, Amanda!" Jakob was insistent. "You bring me something for Richard's headache."

Even Richard caught the dark and menacing hint. He sat on the couch and his muscles ached from constriction. It felt like a dream to him. *It couldn't be possible*, he thought. He wished that he was sleeping and everything was an illusion, but he wasn't and his headache persisted.

The unusual spirit of Maria Prescott spoke again. *"Go my child"* Her head shuddered to Amanda. *"Go, and do as he asks. Get something for him to use for Richard's headache. And don't be too long, you understand, don't you child?"*

Amanda nodded and the forces that were restraining her body, released, and set her free. She slowly walked past Jakob, who watched her carefully, and then side stepped the majestic light before running up the stairs. The rest of the family sighed in relief and wished their sister mental fortitude and good fortune.

"What exactly is happening here, Mrs. Prescott?" The inquisitive Mary, needed an explanation. Jakob, on the other hand, didn't pay any attention. He turned his body to face the bedroom where Donald slept, and waited patiently.

"Your mother and father conceived Jakob in your old house. The old Murphy house. Your father was very sick, my dear."

"Yeah, we get that, Mrs. Prescott, but you cleansed that house. You took the evil away. It was Jimmy Murphy and you took him away." Richard's body remained inadequate, but his speech was relatively unrestricted. After he was finished speaking, some saliva trickled out of his mouth and down his chin, but he was unable to address it, and it landed on the crotch of his pants, camouflaging itself with the beads of sweat dripping from his brow.

"It's what happened before that, Richard. It was the conception that caused this. Before I freed the spirits of the Murphy family and got rid of Jimmy Murphy's energy. The conception transferred the energy into your beautiful mother."

After a short pause, Mary was completely engaged, and requested some more information. "Please, Mrs. Prescott, please tell us more of what you know." Jakob didn't move or even respond to any of the discussion. His focus was steadfast and his confidence was overbearing.

"Your father was sick. This you knew, but your father was sick when he and your mother conceived Jakob. Do you understand? A part of Jimmy Murphy's soul was transferred to your mother, and your brother, Jakob, just inherited it."

Richard turned red in the face. "Ho-wool-e-shit" He took some time to process the treasured information. "That all makes sense guys. Jakob is the spawn of Jimmy Murphy. He's not a Sterling. He's a Murphy…he…he's a Murphy bastard."

"He made a pact with the evil entity. With the residual energy of Jimmy Murphy. It was to be initiated on the boy's seventh birthday and he was

to carry out the actions that the Murphy boy failed to achieve. He needed a vessel to transport his strength and Jakob's DNA contains the very same, selfish, and manipulative persona, as the original host."

Mary joined the shocking exchange. "Oh, please, Mrs. Prescott, you have to stop him from hurting us!"

Jakob slowly turned around, as the wall clock read 11:38 in the evening, and eerily smiled at his oldest sister. He shook his head back and forth, solidifying her utmost fears.

"I can warn you child, and offer you advice. But I'm in the afterlife now, my dear. Your destiny is up to you and you only. I can't help you any longer."

23
Birthday Wishes

July 17, 1987

TECHNICALLY, the cheap plastic clock that dangled on the basement wall hadn't struck midnight yet. But little Jakob Sterling's patience had surrendered to his vicious anger. The troubled boy wasn't awaiting his birthday party. He was just anticipating his permission. He hungered for his irrational and freakish call to action, and now he felt like he was back in charge.

"You should leave now, bad dead lady." Jakob's eye's shimmered and turned a dark greenish colour. "I'm not scared of you and maybe no one else is either dead lady. Just leave now and make your light go away."

"No, Jakob." Mary stopped him, right away. "Why should she leave? You don't have any beef with her do you? She doesn't have to go anywhere, and you really can't do anything about it, can you?"

"She should leave because she's dead. That's why. I've already seen dead Mommy. I don't want to talk to dead Prescott. That's why you should leave now Prescott…cause' you're dead and you don't even have a headache."

The remarkable spectacle of Maria Prescott's spirit was robotic and unemotional. *"Come with me, Jakob. Come with me now, before you create more pain for this family. They don't need your pain Jabob."*

The little boy shook his head, back and forth, and then smirked from ear to ear. "You can leave, lady. You're not sick." Then he had his own frightening realization. *Where did Amanda go?* He wondered. *She was supposed to go and get me something to help out with Richard's headache. She might have run away...*His thoughts raced through his mind in a matter of milliseconds.

As Jakob turned to the staircase, bound and determined to hunt Amanda down and avoid blame for letting her go in the first place, the clock's hands both reached for the ceiling. There would be no difference between this minute, the last minute, and the minute to come, for that matter, but the seventh year had arrived for Jakob, and he knew that it was his time. He stopped and looked up at the clock and then he turned to Mary.

"Mary, is it my birthday now? The clock looks like it does when I have lunch. But I'm not hungry right now."

She was more afraid, at this time in her life, then at any other time. This included all the pain from the Murphy house. Mary tried to stall her brother.

"No, Jakob. Not yet. It'll be your birthday when you get up in the morning, but you have to go to bed first."

Mary remained where she was when Jakob stopped and trapped her. She assumed that her eyes were dry of tears by now, but again, they leaked.

"Mary, remember when you showed me my lesson, in the book? It was a book with numbers and clocks, and you made me draw clock hands, remember?"

"Yes, I do remember, Jakob. Do you want to do that again with me? Let me go and we'll play whatever you want, I promise."

"I remember you showed me when the two hands are standing up together it was lunch time when it was light and midnight when it was dark."

Jakob, Mary, and even Richard, who attempted to turn his neck to an obtuse angle, now feared the worst. He was much smarter than they gave him credit for. They turned to the tiny basement window and the blackness of the night screamed. Mary knew that she had been caught in a lie and before her little brother's next moves, she urinated through her blue jeans, causing a dark, yellow puddle on the lacklustre basement floor.

"Ohhhh, poor Mary," Jakob mocked the embarrassed Sterling woman. "Maybe you need a diaper, Mary." Jakob pinched his nose and turned back toward the bedroom to handle his task, once and for all.

Mary and Richard yelled at Jakob as he approached the doorway to Donald's bedroom. The cries for assistance and warnings toward their father fell on deaf ears. The heavy bedroom door suddenly slammed shut in front of the youngster, but Jakob only hesitated, turning to Maria Prescott's bright vision and smiling, paying tribute to her supernatural efforts.

Jakob entered the room before closing the door and locking it behind him. There would be no more delays. No one to save the patriarch of the family now. Donald had stirred from the noises, but was still far too inebriated to function properly. He lay on his chest and his face was turned, allowing him to breathe.

Little Jakob got up on the bed and removed the rope from around his waist. He put the rod down for a moment and gently collected Donald's hands, after folding his arms behind him. He took the rope and tied a simple hitch knot, pulling it tight at the end and dropping his father's arms back onto his body. He reached down and picked up the rod, twirling it in his little hands, and positioning his body straight over his father's head. He could hear the others, outside the locked door, screaming for Amanda now. But they were still restrained. *Where was Amanda? She will be too late to save him...*

Realizing that both ends of the rotisserie skewer had sharp, pointed ends on it, Jakob peered around the room for something to shield his tiny hand. His eyes were now adjusting to the darkness.

Mary had taken her father's shoes and socks off. One of the rolled up socks sat on the floor by the corner of the bed and Jakob bounced over to it and picked it up. He assumed his previous position and clutched the crumpled sock in his right hand. He held the metal rod tight, using the sock as padding and grip. After placing his left hand a little bit lower, Jakob looked directly down, onto his father's head.

"You are so sick, Donald. Now you will be too sick to breathe," he whispered, almost respecting Donald's extreme drowsiness.

Amanda had finally returned and hammered on the door with both of her fists. She screamed and her cries blended in with the others. She was too late and the guilt was already eating away at her soul. She had been held up by the police on the telephone. They wouldn't let her go back downstairs until they arrived. She couldn't wait any longer, but it was too late. They were all too late.

The unstable, little Sterling boy raised the steel rod high above his head, and without remorse, released his entire body weight down, toward Donald. The barbeque rod entered just below the ear lobe and continued through, penetrating the top of his neck. Blood splashed in all directions and Jakob pushed with all of his might, as Donald's body rocked up and down from the trauma. There was little sound from the Sterling father. Jakob finished the job by pumping his arms and jamming the rod further and further into Donald's head.

Donald's lifeless body defecated on the sheets; it was surrounded by a bright red splatter of blood droplets. Jakob leaned on the steel bar, even fiercer, and eventually it fully exited through the top of Donald's neck, albeit just an inch or so. Donald Sterling was most definitely dead, and Jakob had finally claimed one of his prizes. Now the scene had become disturbing and Jakob would certainly thrive in his element. The boy sneezed from his adrenalin and smeared some droplets of blood on his face with his arm.

Outside the bedroom, everyone had quieted down. Jakob put his ear against the door and could hear the low frequency of Maria Prescott's energy, as well as, Mary's whimpering. He sluggishly unlocked the door and walked away from the brutal murder scene.

He was covered in his father's blood, but the lights had been turned off by Amanda so it was too dark to make out anyone except for the brilliant Maria Prescott. Jakob was well aware that his traumatised victims would still be immobilized, so he rubbed at his eyes and wore Donald's blood on his face like war paint.

"Richard? Donald's stupid headache is finally gone." Mary whimpered louder and it allowed Jakob to gain perspective of his location in the room. "Now I can help you so your headache can go away too, and then you won't need to breathe anymore."

It had appeared that Jimmy Murphy, through the body of Jakob Sterling, had finally won the war. A senseless, meaningless, petty and costly war, in which Jimmy Murphy started himself, but another was bound and determined to finish so he could hold his trophy's high.

Amanda sensed her brother's position. She ran toward his voice and clenched her eyes and teeth. She gripped the shiny silver handle of the largest frying pan that she had found in the kitchen. When she sensed that she was the proper distance from her little brother, she swung the pan, awkwardly, and caught Jakob on the edge of his chin, knocking him to the ground. His body began to aggressively convulse and he yelped like a bear in a steel trap.

Amanda bounced around with the frying pan in both hands, swinging widely and catching nothing but air. But now she was coming dangerously close to her sister's face, and just before she made a regretful mistake, she stopped swinging and ran back the way that she came, flicking on the light and revealing the chaotic environment around her. The ghost of Maria Prescott bowed her head.

Jakob became quiet and lay unconscious on the floor. Richard and Mary were still frozen and this prompted advice from the spirit of Maria Prescott.

"He's not dead yet. You must finish him off or he'll never stop pursuing you. You will regret your poor decision, once and for all."

Amanda looked down at Jakob. He had their father's blood strewn across him and now his own plasma, leaking from his chin and mouth. She knew that her father was gone. She didn't even need to confirm it. The other two knew it as well. It was obvious, and they couldn't run to his aid anyway. The silence from the bedroom compelled them to save their breath from screaming, and it had become hoarse from their previous attempts anyway.

The youngest Sterling girl, nearly a woman herself, walked over to the sofa where Richard sat and grabbed a throw pillow from the side. She turned young Jakob over, onto his back, and he began to babble. He had come to and his little eyes opened slightly and displayed a calming shade of green, frosted over with tears. Amanda started breathing heavier and her vision was fogged by a powerful combination of make-up and her emotions.

She raised the pillow above her head and Jakob's gurgle turned into a slight snarl. As he tried to recover, his alleged pain didn't even make him cry out for help. As jakob pouted his bottom lip and beseeched forgiveness from his youngest sister, Amanda placed the pillow, gently on Jakob's face, restricting his oxygen and causing the boy to struggle. He kicked his legs and a fearful groaning sound was overheard from underneath the pillow.

Once Jakob's feet had stopped twitching, Amanda slowly lifted the pillow and the rest all cried and wailed. A couple of seconds after Jakob's demise, Mary and Richard were released from their imprisonment. Richard was nauseous and cried on the chesterfield while Mary ran into the bedroom to discover the horrific scene.

"Well, Jakob, you are a powerless young man. Now you will come with me, like I told you to, in the first place. The evil place is waiting for you, Jimmy, and now you can finally rest in peace."

A dark mass rose high above the body of Jakob Sterling. It hovered in one place for a moment, but in perfect timing to the shivering and frightening shrieks, from Mary, in the bedroom, it floated sideways, picking up speed, and quickly disappeared into the translucent body of Maria Prescott's ghostly figure.

"Mrs. Prescott!" Amanda cried at the thought of her father, but her feelings flooded to her deceased mother and whether or not she would ever see her bright smile again. "Will you please say hello to my mother? She hasn't visited me in many months and I'm so afraid for her." Mary's screams continued and now Richard had joined his sister at the ghastly sight. "Tell her I love her... please?"

After a short pause, Maria Prescott's apparition made her last point short. "I'm not in your mother's world, my dear. You will have to wake her and tell her yourself." And it was at that time that the brilliant energy faded away and, without emotion and without any goodbyes, she was gone.

Amanda ran into the bedroom and screeched with her siblings. The pain was traumatising and difficult to believe, but any doubt was soon forgotten by the dire message, written in blood, and strewn across the room. Each of them stood in a circle around their father's lifeless body.

The shiny metal rod had penetrated Donald's head and extruded from the other side of his neck. And he had no arms. They were tied behind his back. It was just like the mysterious picture. Jakob wasn't drawing the man's arms going through his head. They weren't his arms at all. This had been his plan from the beginning. He was programmed from birth and forced into a murderous existence. In the end, Jakob Sterling never really stood a chance to exist innocently.

And now he was gone. Far too early by any stranger's opinion, but his victims would surely disagree. His victims included his mother, his father, his dog, and his twin brother. They were never given a chance to fight back. His size fooled the masses and their regret would come far too late. Jakob Sterling had created his own fearsome legacy.

Richard had lost all of his composure and collapsed onto the bed, lying in his father's desiccating body fluids. Amanda too, was devastated. She couldn't imagine life without either of her parents, and cried uncontrollably. And Mary couldn't believe the fatal outcome. Her agony was unbearable and she was in obvious shock. She reached down and removed the rope from Donald's arms, her despair commanding the room.

Mary's terrifying cries were heard by all, but it seemed as if no one was listening. Most obvious though, was the one who wasn't able to, Donald Sterling. His demise would leave a hole, far too deep to crawl out of. And as the responding officers entered the once innocent house, Mary slobbered and couldn't stop herself from yelling down at her father's lifeless body.

"Daddy? Daddy? Please wake up, Daddy. Please don't leave us. Don't leave me, Daddy! Wake up…wake up Daddy, wake up…wake up." *Wake up…wake up…wake up…wake up…*

24
A Premonition of Epic Proportions

July 17, 1980

"WAKE up! Wake up! Wake up! You have to wake up now, sweetheart. I know that you're tired, but you have to be strong now. You have a baby to deliver, try and stay awake now, okay, honey? As long as I'm here, you're gonna be safe."

"Donald, I've just had a horrible dream! No… no, it was a nightmare, really."

Donald leaned over his wife. "It was just a dream, Barb. Don't worry about that stuff now. You have to concentrate on your breathing. Is the pain still bothering you like it was earlier?"

"Donald, the dream was about Jimmy Murphy."

"Jimmy Murphy? Donald hesitated and anxiety crossed his face. "Why are you thinking about Jimmy Murphy, Barb? His evil is behind us, once and for all. There's no reason to fear him any longer."

"Wait…wait. Donald, something isn't right. I've been here before. We've had this conversation before, a long, long time ago."

Donald was puzzled. "What are you talking about, honey? Please, try and relax."

"No, Donald, you really don't understand. Something horrible is about to happen. There's more than-"

Donald interrupted her, "Stop it now, Barbara. Forget about Jimmy Murphy and concentrate on this special little gift that you're bringing into this world. Jimmy Murphy is a thing of the past and so is that evil energy that interfered with our lives."

Barbara managed to speak up again, despite her medicated state. "You realize, that it's almost been three years, to the day, that Richard had his accident?" And with that news, Barbara began to hyperventilate.

"Breathe slower, Barb. Breathe slower. You're going to be alright. You just need to keep breathing normal. You've done this before, Barb, you're a fighter. Don't ever forget how special you are to me and the kids." Donald felt very light headed and his eyes periodically glazed over with tiny black dots. Barbara began to breathe ordinarily again, but opened her mouth wide, and cried out in pain.

Doctor Collins met the medical personnel at reception and barked orders at the paramedics to take Mrs. Sterling, immediately, to operating room number two. He motioned for Donald to wait outside of the room and charged in, followed by three nurses and an intern. Donald watched through the window at the top of the door as the specialists transferred his struggling wife onto the delivery table and began preparing sharp needles and supplies to comfort her. Another nurse approached the door and asked Donald to move aside, but he made a quick gesture and stopped her by holding out his arm, demanding an answer.

"I need you to tell me what's going on. Please, you need to tell me if my wife is going to be okay. What's happening in there? Is there something that you're not telling me? Now isn't the time for secrets."

"Please, sir," the nurse pleaded, "let me through. I can't tell you the status of Mrs. Sterling if you don't allow me to pass."

Donald thought quickly about his actions and pulled back his arm, allowing the nurse to enter the room. She certainly understood his concern so she hesitated and tried to give him some comfort.

"Please, Mr. Sterling, have a seat over there and the doctor will give you an update as soon as possible." She swung open the door and rushed over to Barbara.

After twenty-two minutes, Doctor Collins came out of Barbara's room and approached the concerned husband.

"Mr. Sterling." He reached out his hand to guide Donald away from the small crowd. "Please, come with me. I have an update for you. Let's go somewhere a bit more private, if you don't mind."

The two men walked around the corner and into an empty hallway.

"Mr. Sterling… do you mind if I call you Donald?" He waited for the worried husband's approval and continued. "Donald, Barbara has been sedated. She's in early labour and actually has the urge to push already, but we've given her something to combat that. She's sleeping rather comfortably for the moment. I would suggest that we let her rest for an hour or so. Do you have something that you need to take care of? Barbara was asking about the kids. Go and see them, Donald."

"What about the baby, doctor? How's the baby? Barbara is really worried about the baby." *As she should be.*

"The baby seems quite fine. We're all hearing a nice strong heartbeat and it doesn't seem to be in any distress at the moment. Go and see your family. Bring the children back with you in an hour or so. I'll be able to give you some more news then, okay?"

An hour had swiftly passed since Donald left his wife to pick up his kids. The family had just entered through the emergency doors when Doctor Collins intercepted them and pulled Donald away from his children.

"Donald, something peculiar has happened."

Donald peered at the doctor and then scanned the room, looking for answers. "What's peculiar, doctor? What do you mean?"

"Barbara woke up, Donald. We sedated her, but she woke up hysterical. She was screaming your name at first, like she was having a nightmare or something like that. Then she started up again and she was blaring 'Jimmy…Jimmy…Jimmy!' It was quite concerning to everyone in the hospital, but then she calmed down and asked for you and the children again."

"Can I see her? Can we all go in and see her? She needs her family right now."

"Yes, you can go and see her now, but not for long. You should know that we've given your wife an epidural. She's completely numb from her waist down to ease her pain. The delivery is imminent." *The physical pain was easy to conceal, but the mental pain was too transparent to hide.*

In single file, the family made their way to Barbara's room and opened the door where she lay motionless on the bed. She cracked a smile and her eye's widened at the site of her cherished ones. Unfortunately, Barbara had something on her mind and it plagued her thoughts.

"Oh, thank God you're all here! You have to listen to me. Everything is happening to me, just like in the crazy nightmare that I had. It's exactly the same. Please, you've got to get me out of here, Donald. You and the kids are in great danger. The baby is evil guys. The baby is evil. Please you have to listen to me for a minute. You have to listen to me!"

"Don't worry yourself, honey." Donald tried to comfort his wife. "They know exactly what they're doing here. You're going to be just fine." He repeated these words to her over and over; it made Barbara feel sick to her stomach, but she never let on. She remained as strong as she possibly could, for her children.

"Yeah, Mom, you're going to be back on your feet in no time," Richard spoke up. "Like Dad says. Soon it'll be all over and we can go back home with our new brother or sister. Is there anything that we can get for you, Mom?"

Every word that left Richard's mouth had been spoken before. Barbara felt conspired against and confirmed that her nightmare was coming true, right in front of her eyes.

"No! I don't need anything except to get out of this damn hospital! Something horrendous is about to happen to me! You guys have to listen to me."

"Mommy," Amanda interjected, "why do you think something is going to happen to you? Your baby won't let anything happen to you. The baby will protect you."

After shaking her head and mentally trying to slow her heartbeat down, Barbara clenched her fists and confessed in great detail.

"There's two babies. One won't make it. Jakob… Jakob… he's got Jimmy Murphy in him, Donald. Jakob. I'm going to die. I'm going to die…please."

"Who's Jakob, Barbara? What are you talking about?" Donald appeared to have absolutely no idea. "Enough with Jimmy Murphy, Barbara! I told you, it's not healthy for the baby. That bloody kid has caused enough bullshit."

Mary leaned in to her mother. "You are the strongest woman that I know, Mom. Everything I've ever learned about being a good big sister, I've learned from you."

"Mary!" Barbara tried to reach the sanity of anyone who would listen. "Don't let this happen. I'm so scared. You have to make it stop! He's evil, Mary. He's evil and he wants to get all of you. It'll be when he's seven years old. Exactly on his seventh birthday. Please, don't let this happen."

It was about then that Richard Sterling looked up to the ceiling tiles and felt an overwhelming queasiness, which was accompanied by an instantaneous and throbbing headache.

The lights in the hospital room flickered and everyone looked up toward them. No sooner had a nurse come in to the room when Barbara let out a dreadful scream and arched her neck toward the ceiling. The heart monitor that was hooked up to Barbara started beeping and panic ensued throughout the room.

"Donald," the doctor barked at the confused husband, "you all have to leave the room now."

"I'm not going anywhere, God dammit, my wife needs me." Donald was standing his ground as Barbara's delicate condition continued to deteriorate.

The doctor commanded, "Nurse Johnston, please take Mr. Sterling out and scrub him for surgery. You'll just make her sicker Donald. Go with the nurse."

Once Donald returned, sterile and clothed for surgery, he ran to his wife's bedside once again. She was barely conscious, but managed to open her eyes enough to look at her husband. He cupped his wife's hand in his own and smiled at her. His very presence seemed to offer a level of relaxation to his disheveled wife.

"You're right here," she said in a whisper, "Something is wrong, Donald. I can't feel anything. I'm numb all over."

"The nurses have made you comfortable, Barb. Soon we will have our new addition. Hang in there, honey."

Barbara used what energy and strength that she had left to try, one last time, to beseech some understanding from her husband. If there was a time she needed his devotion, it was now.

"Donald, do you remember when you were sick? You were really angry with me and I calmed you down. We made love that night, Donald. Do you remember that? You caressed my thigh, and you know how I liked it and you kissed me behind my ear, just like you used to when we were first going out together. We made love and it was truly magical. It was exactly what we both needed to escape from the sadness and the anger, for just a short period of time, anyway. But you were sick, Donald. And you passed your evil sickness onto this baby. Onto *these* babies, actually. One will die Donald, and the other will be sick too. Just like you were when we made love. He will be so sick that he'll cause more pain and devastation to our family."

Donald listened attentively, with a sheepish grin on his face and an empathetic look in his eyes. It really didn't even matter what she said next. *But he listened...*

"I already told you, Donald. I'm going to die. The baby will destroy me on the way out. He wants you and Richard, Donald. He wants to make you his new victims. And he wants the girls too. You're all in trouble. I'm trying to warn you."

The enigmatic husband stroked his wife's hand and his eyes glossed over from the reflective light in the room, showing a yellowish flush. Donald appeared defeated, but he licked his lips and smiled attentively.

"He's going to get you, Donald. He's going to take your life, right in front of the children. You have to stop it from happening, honey.... please. Just take me out of here. I don't want to be here anymore."

A few more tears trickled from her tired eyes and they triggered an extraordinary sensation in her mind. Her legs were numb and she felt each and every tear as it rolled down her face, like the carving of a razor-sharp blade, cutting her deeply.

Donald slowly let go of his loving wife's hand and walked around the delivery table. *Around and around.* It seemed like, at least ten times to Barbara, who was starting to lose consciousness. Returning to her side, he looked directly into her eyes and smiled while his surgical mask rested below his chin. It was a smile that Barbara hadn't seen in ages. *Or maybe ever...*

"Barbara, my dear, you don't have to worry about any of that garbage right now. Everything is going to turn out just fine, honey. It always does."

Thank you for your contribution

I need to recognize, seven year old, Tait Christenson. Tait was the winner of a social media contest that I held on my personal page. I received more than twenty submissions and found out, quickly, that I would have my work cut out for me to pick a winner. Each and every child that entered my contest was a good looking boy. Well cared for and morally strong, by first glance.

But something about Tait kept training my eye to his image while deciding. His eyes, his hair, and his innocence is what compelled me to choose him and he didn't let me down. He appeared, with his father, at the photo shoot and was on his best behaviour. So motivated to do a great job. It was such a pleasure to meet Tait Christenson and his image will forever be branded as the face of Jakob Sterling.

Also: Matthew Broughton, Ross Christenson, Kevin Williams, Sandra Blackwell, Deanna Kersey, Stacie Rae, and Stephen King. Your assistance and/or motivation were key to the completion of this project. I so greatly appreciate your contributions on this magical journey and I certainly can't thank you enough. Please continue sharing your insights and helping me achieve my dreams.

About the Author

STEVEN Blackwell lives in Alberta, Canada with his wife, Sandra and two teenage children, David and Alicia. He and his family members inadvertently became the four main characters in his first book, *232 Birch*, which shares an extraordinary and real life, paranormal depiction. Since then, the subject of the supernatural has enticed Steven to research and share his imagination about the paranormal. Publishing his first, full length novel, in 2016, *The Pale Murphys*, Steven continues to dabble with the increasing curiosities of the genre, and introduces his thrilling and emotional sequel, *Jakob Sterling*. The future offers endless possibilities for Steven's next projects and he continually looks forward to sharing his creative imagination with his readers.